CARTY

CARTY

GARDNER F. FOX

DOUBLEDAY & COMPANY, INC.
GARDEN CITY, NEW YORK
1977

All of the characters in this book are fictitious,
and any resemblance to actual persons,
living or dead, is purely coincidental.

ISBN: 0-385-12866-5
Library of Congress Catalog Card Number 77–76238

CARTY

CHAPTER 1

He eased the horse across the little stream and up the far
bank, sitting easy in the kak against the tiredness flooding
his rawboned body. He had been riding since before
sunup, with a far piece yet to go, and death waiting for
him at the end of his riding. He had accepted this fact
long ago, was grown used to it by this time.

He wore a deerskin shirt outside his Levi's, heavily
fringed and stained with the long rubbing of his heavy
shellbelt. From the shirt he took papers and tobacco and
built himself a smoke, letting the smoke ease down into
his lungs, vaguely soothing, as his eyes roamed the grasslands ahead of him.

Amos Carty did not want to die; he was not ready to be
pushed into a pine box and shoved down into six feet of
hard earth. The wind that stirred the long yellow hair
under his low-crowned Plains hat was filled with a fragrance of sage and greasewood; it told him life was all
around him, to be lived at its fullest, and that only a bullet waited for him at Stovepipe.

Carty smiled thinly.

He had made a promise. He would keep it.

The grulla horse made good time with its loping stride,
leaving the buttes and malpais behind them, heading
straight across the grama grass. To one side, on a slope to
the east, a stretch of ground was covered over with the
small yellow flowers of the maguey bushes growing there.

The rider flicked his eyes toward them, letting memory carry him backward.

As a boy he had worked over plants like that, down in Kiowa country where he had grown up, stripping the leaves from them, gathering the sweet syrup from their flowers. The Kiowas had made a drink from that syrup, had eaten the tender insides of the leaves. He had lived ten years of his life with them, before the father who had abandoned him had come to claim him.

Amos Carty stirred. Sometimes he felt more Indian than white; it was a matter of that early training, ingrained into his very nature was their mistrust of white men. He smiled at that, but it was true.

He had trusted Ken Stevens.

And because Stevens had violated that trust, he was going to die.

His shoulders lifted in a faint shrug. Everybody had to die, some time. Maybe that was the Indian in him; he was imbued with their fatalism. Well, he had also learned honor from old Buffalo Horn.

He had given his word.

And so he was riding now, to Stovepipe.

No map showed the location of Stovepipe. It was somewhere up there in the Horseheads, a collection of three buildings, maybe four, where not many men lived but where those who rode the long trail came to stop, knowing themselves safe from the law.

Morgan Chance was waiting in Stovepipe. For him, Carty.

He would have his men with him, hard-bitten longriders who would as soon throw down on him without warning as not, if Morg Chance said the word. He wondered whether he would be allowed to ride into town or be cut down somewhere on its outskirts, where one or two riflemen would be hidden behind the big rocks that fronted the one trail into and out of Stovepipe.

Well, no matter. Except that he would have relished a chance to defend himself with his Colt or Spencer rifle. He didn't want to die like a mad dog, shot down without warning. Anger stirred in him, then faded. Of what use was anger? His had been the choice to come here, because he had given his word. He doubted even that Morg Chance really expected him.

He smiled thinly, picturing Morg's surprise. Might be he would be able to ride into Stovepipe, if that were the case. And if he rode into Stovepipe alive, he wouldn't be the only man to die.

His hands moved to the walnut-butted Colt in its worn leather holster, loosening it. Then he chuckled, shaking his head.

"*Pei, pei,*" he muttered in Kiowan. "That's what I am. Spooked."

He rode on, pushing aside his thoughts and his memories.

He touched the grulla with a toe, urging him to greater speed. The sooner at Stovepipe, the sooner over. The grama grass was behind him now, he was moving up into the foothills, in among the clumps of juniper, the tall pines. The air seemed somehow cleaner here, with a bite of melting snow in the wind.

The grulla was climbing steadily along a narrow path. To his right a stand of quaking aspens rustled where the wind touched the silver-tipped leaves, and up ahead the lodgepole pines began their march to the high peaks, like sentinels. The air was colder, bracing, and only the sunlight gave warmth upon his shoulders.

Rocks lay sprawled off to one side, remnants of a fault a long time ago that had split the mountainside and left that debris in its wake. Men could hide among those rocks, but Carty did not believe they did. It was too soon, too early. Chance would want to gloat a little before he gave the orders to shoot.

He might be wrong. He thought about that, swaying in the worn Cheyenne saddle. Yes, he could be wrong. But he did not think so. Morg would enjoy holding the winning hole card on him, being that sort of man.

The climbing here was steep, though the grulla did not labor. The mouse-colored horse was a good one; it had speed and endurance. Carty had fought an Osage for the horse in an Indian encampment, two years before. Like as not, the Osage had stolen it off a rancher. The Osages were great horse thieves. Not as good as the Kiowas or the Comanches, but good enough.

Sunlight touched metal, up above.

He knew it was a rifle barrel. Morg Chance had a man up there, watching the trail. Carty laid his gaze across the rimrocks, but he did not tense, feeling certain that Morg Chance would want to put eyes on him, to savor the moment before the bullets would plow into him.

And that might be Chance's big mistake.

Carty let the grulla break into a canter when it came to a level stretch. Not so far, now. Another climb between the lodgepoles and he would be on the final level, be able to see the town itself.

In among the pines, he was safe enough. Nobody would try to shoot through those branches at him. His hand went to the Colt out of long habit. It would not be a rifle that would bring him down, but handguns. And with handguns he had a mite better than an even chance.

He came to the level and reined in, sitting the grulla almost lazily, pausing to build a smoke, letting his hands perform the movements even as his stare went on before him. Four buildings, then. Shacks, really. Wind-whipped and sunbaked, leaning a little, it seemed. A general store and a saloon, something that might be called a boardinghouse, and a blacksmith shop with a livery stable. The men who rode to Stovepipe would need little more. Not here, anyhow.

He saw no sign of life except for half a dozen horses tied to the hitchrail before the saloon. There were others in the livery stable, he felt certain. Morg Chance always had a large number of gunmen around him.

Carty waited patiently, easing his seat in the kak. There was at least one rifleman behind him, high in the rimrocks. There might be others. Thus far they had made no move. He heeled the grulla forward at a walk.

The hooffalls of the horse started up puffs of dust and made soft sounds. Carty took a last drag of his cigarette and let it slip from his fingers. His eyes were on the saloon, but he did not ignore the livery stable nor the boardinghouse.

He walked the length of the little main street to the tierail and there he sat, waiting, wondering a little. His Colt was easy to get at, loose and ready.

A man opened the batwing doors and came out onto the little porch, squinting a little against the late-afternoon sunlight. He was a medium-sized man with broad shoulders, wearing a faded red flannel shirt and heavy shellbelt. His face was triangular, and Carty thought, as he had a while back when he had ridden with this man, that his eyes were set too close together.

"Hobe," Carty said into the silence.

Hobe Talbert let his lips slide into a smile. There was no mirth in that smile, nor in his words as he said, "You come. By God, you come. I'd never have believed it."

"You're not a believing man, Hobe. Always was too suspicious."

Talbert nodded, his grin fading. He frowned, holding

his head sideways. "I lost money on you, Indian. A double eagle. To Morg."

"Morg bet on a sure thing, Hobe."

"Did he? I don't get that."

Carty shook his head, eased his leg over the cantle, and came down onto the dusty street. Talbert was standing easily, with no threat in him, and that was strange. Or maybe Morg Chance wasn't going to do this one man against another but was waiting until he had his whole force siding him.

Talbert moved sideways a step or two. "Come on in. Morg's been expecting you."

Carty moved forward, up the two steps and onto the porch, alert against any play Talbert might make. But the other man was standing easily, not moving, his thumbs hooked in his gunbelt. He lifted his left hand and waved it at the batwings.

"After you, Indian."

Carty pushed against wood, stepped into what seemed like darkness after all that sunlight. His eyes adjusted quickly. Three men were lined up at the bar, elbows resting on it. Carty knew two of them, Pike Shattuck and Ed Wells.

At a table to one side, close by a window that looked down at the trail, a big man sat with a pack of soiled cards in his hands. His hair was black and long; a drooping mustache framed a thin mouth. His calfskin vest held a gold watchchain, and Carty noticed that his boots were new and carefully polished, which surprised him a little.

"You owe me twenty, Hobe," Chance said softly.

Chance chuckled as Talbert cursed. Then his leg kicked a chair toward Carty. "Sit yourself, Amos. Might as well be comfortable."

His arm lifted toward the bar. "Still drinking fire-water?"

"When it's safe."

Morgan Chance boomed laughter. He seemed very pleased with himself as he put the cards face down on the table and leaned back. He took tobacco and papers from his vest pocket and made a cigarette. His eyes never left Carty.

"Go on, Indian. Sit yourself."

Carty was puzzled. He knew Morg Chance was not a man to forget an injury, nor to forgive one. Ken Stevens had stolen money Morg figured belonged to him. Carty had told Chance he would go surety for Ken Stevens, who was not a thief. In his eyes, Stevens must have felt the money belonged to him and not to Morgan Chance.

He waited until the barkeep came with two glasses and set them down, one for him, one for Chance. Then he pulled the chair toward him and rested himself.

The play would come, he knew this. The man across the table from him was savoring the moment, relishing the power he held over Amos Carty. He was testing his triumph as he was even now sipping from the glass, slowly and with pleasure. His face was crinkled from his grin.

"Seen Stevens lately?" Morg asked.

Carty shook his head. "Not for months. I've been riding the back trails."

"But you heard he wasn't coming?"

"I heard."

A man in dusty clothes had appeared out of nowhere one morning, riding up on him as he was breaking his camp in San Carlos country, had dismounted and shared a tin cup of coffee with him. The man had talked, had told him news of one thing and another, all the way from

Eagle Pass to Ogallala, and in the talking, had mentioned
Ken Stevens and how he had cut his rope and drifted
west into California.

Carty had known then that he would ride to Stovepipe
to meet this man across the table from him. He had been
bitterly disappointed in Ken Stevens; it didn't seem like
something Stevens would do.

Morg pushed the empty whiskey glass across the table,
never taking his eyes from Carty. There was something in
those eyes, or behind them inside his brain, that Carty
could not lay a finger to. He got the feeling that he would
not like what he would see, if he could.

"I came, like I said."

"Expecting death?"

"A fight, at least."

Chance chuckled. "Hope I'm not disappointing you, Indian."

His men laughed around the room. Carty felt the relax-
ation all through him. For the first time, it occurred to
him that maybe Morgan Chance didn't want him dead,
after all; but he wanted something from him that he
couldn't lay a hand on.

"A man is never disappointed to know he's going to
live."

"I didn't say that."

The words were like cold water in his face. Carty
tensed, but could find no threat in this smiling man across
from him. Would Chance dare to wave his gunmen at
him, here? When he himself stood to die first, from
Carty's gun? Not likely, not at all.

"You're worse than an Apache trying to hide his sign,"
Carty said softly. "You ever trailed an Apache who didn't
want to be found, Morg? You bust a gut at the job, and
nine times out of ten you don't succeed. You're like that
now. You got something to say, say it."

Morgan Chance nodded. "You got a choice, Carty. You do what I ask, and you ride out of here a free man, beholden to nobody, especially me. You refuse, and maybe you will die here, after all."

Carty stared at him, wondering. What was so important to Morgan Chance that he would bring Amos Carty across six hundred miles of sunbaked ground? Carty was a gunfighter, almost an outlaw. He kept much to himself, he rode the back trails and the high hills, and in his going, he rarely mingled with the men at the ranches or at the forts. Not even in the towns.

"You're still dragging a rope behind you, Morg."

"I got enemies, Indian."

"Who doesn't?"

"Bad enemies. I don't mean just some lawman who might try to make a rep by coming after me. You ever heard of Nogales Jack? Or Rawhide Bledsoe?"

"Met them some years back, over in Durango. They were hiding out, then. Matter of a whiskey-selling to the Osages."

Chance nodded his big head. "They took an interest in a lot of things."

"And now they've taken an interest in you."

The black eyes glinted. As though he were uncomfortable, Morgan Chance shifted in his chair. His hand went to the calfskin vest and lifted out a gold watch. He clicked it, the cover came up, and he glanced down at the dial.

"I got enemies, Indian. I also got a sister."

Carty sighed. "Didn't know that."

"She ain't like me; she's a good girl."

Carty shrugged. It was of no moment to him. But Chance scowled, seeing the gesture, and snarled a little.

"A good girl, Carty," he repeated.

"I'm listening."

"Man wants to marry her, over in the Mogollon country. Rich man, got a fine ranch. Twenty, thirty thousand head."

"That's a big ranch, all right."

"I want her to marry that man, Indian."

Amos Carty spread his hands. "I'm not stopping her."

Chance grinned, wolfishly. "No. You're helping her."

It was not often that Amos Carty allowed himself to be surprised. He was surprised now. He came halfway off his chair, his eyes locked onto those of Morgan Chance, and he let the air out of his lungs, very slowly.

"Nogales Jack? Bledsoe?" he asked.

Morgan Chance nodded, biting his lower lip. "They know about it and they sent word there'd be no wedding."

Carty smiled. "You got a small army here, Morg. You just ride to that there ranch and you see your sister married. No two men are going to stop you."

"There'll be more'n the two of them. They've gone and hired gunhands. At least half a dozen of them. They're waiting, Indian. Waiting for me. And for Kate."

Carty shook his head. "Morg, there's more to it than that. Are you asking me to hire on as another gun? Is that it?"

"Just you, Indian. Just you."

"There you go again, covering up your sign."

Chance leaned forward. There was an intentness in him, a desperation, that Carty could sense. For all his bigness, his muscles, his way with guns, Morgan Chance was a man in need.

"You're the only one can do it, Indian."

"Do what?"

"Get Kate safe to that ranch."

Carty looked at the glass on the table that held the

whiskey he had not as yet tasted. There was no thirst in him for whiskey, not ever. He would have preferred cold mountain water to any whiskey ever made. Maybe it was because he had seen what whiskey could do to brave Kiowa men, back when he had been a youngster.

No matter for whys and wherefores.

His hand lifted the glass and he drank. He put the glass down empty and looked straight at Morgan Chance.

"There's more to it than what you say. What can one man do against seven or eight?"

Chance grinned. "Avoid them."

Well, he could do that, all right. If he wanted to stay hidden, no man except maybe an Apache or a Kiowa would find him. Not any white man, certainly.

"With a woman?" he asked reflectively.

"It's the only way, Carty. You think I haven't sweated this all out in my head, night after night? You're the only man I know can do it."

Carty scowled. "Suppose they find us?"

Chance nodded. "I'd rather have you siding her than anybody I know. Even so, even against all seven or eight of them."

"You're mad, Morg."

A metallic sound made Carty tense. Somebody was cocking a gun behind him. He looked at Chance and said, "You aren't going to make a play for me now, are you?"

The other man scowled and muttered, "Put that gun away, Hobe. Honestly, I don't know what you use for brains. Or," he went on slowly, "did you figure on having the Indian do what you've maybe been thinking of doing, lately?"

"Just checking to see if the gun was loaded, boss."

Carty heard the gun being pushed back into its holster. He had been tensed to draw and fire. He could get one man before he died with a bullet in his back. That one man would have been Morgan Chance. Chance knew this. Maybe Hobe Talbert did, too.

Chance kept his eyes on the man behind Carty, but his hand went to his Roskopf watch. Again he glanced down at it. It was an expensive watch; Morgan Chance prided himself on it.

He said heavily, "Kate should be up by now."

His black eyes touched Carty. "She was lying down, like I told her to do. It was a long ride from Fort Bliss. She'll be here soon. I want you to meet her, get acquainted."

He closed the watch lid with a snap. His lips twisted into a grin. "That is, if you want to live out the day?"

Carty smiled faintly. "You'd trust me with her, would you?"

Chance heaved a great sigh, and relief went through him visibly. He lifted the glass and tossed it through the air to one of his men. The bartender filled it; the man brought it back and put it before him.

"The only one I would, Indian," he said at last, softly.

Carty considered that, turning it around in his mind. He was a gunfighter, he used his gun for wages when they were offered, and he was good with his gun. Very good. But it was not so much as a gunman that Morgan Chance wanted him, but as a guide. An Indian guide.

When he wanted, Amos Carty could cross a countryside, and no man would know when or where he had passed. His Kiowa teachers had done a good job with him. It would take an Apache to find any part of his trail when he wanted to hide it. And having found that part, he would not be able to follow it.

But—with a woman?

Carty shook his head. "There will be problems."

"None you can't solve."

"We'll need grub. Pack horses."

Morgan Chance grinned. "I've thought of all that. It's been arranged. All you need to do is take her."

"I might pull out, leave her on her own."

"You came here, didn't you? When it was only your word brought you. You won't leave her." Chance grinned wolfishly. "You'll do your damndest to get her to the Chessboard ranch, Amos. No man could ask any more."

There was a step on the porch. Carty heard the swing of the batwings. He turned his head and stiffened.

She stood just inside the doorway, with the dying sunlight forming a nimbus around her long brown hair, her bloused shoulders, her riding skirt. She came forward, and now Carty could see that her eyes were brown. Her face was the most beautiful he had ever seen.

Kate Chance walked with a swinging stride, but there was a hesitancy in her manner. Her gaze went from her brother to Amos Carty, and she studied him dubiously. Good reason for her to frown, he thought. He was dusty from his long riding, he needed a wash and a shave. To his surprise, he found that he was standing.

"You're the man they've been expecting," she murmured.

There was no need for an answer. He merely looked at her. It was her brother who said, with amusement in his voice, "He's the only one can do the job, Kate."

"Is he an outlaw, too?"

Morgan Chance scratched his stubbled chin. It was not a question usually asked of a man in frontier towns, not being considered polite. As her brother hesitated, Carty smiled.

"There's no price on my head, ma'am."

Her eyes were very steady on him. Carty got the notion

that she was weighing him on invisible scales. Finally she gave a brief little nod.

"All right, Morgan. When do we leave?"

Her brother slapped the table with a hand. The sound was loud in the silence. Tension eased out of him, and he grinned as he looked around the room.

"Sit down, Kate. We can talk now."

She took a chair he pushed forward, and sat between her brother and Carty. There was a quiet watchfulness about her, and Carty sensed she was uneasy under her calm manner. She did not relish this meeting in a back-trail town; she was used to finer things. A man could tell that just by looking at her.

Carty said against her stare, "Sometimes we have to do things we don't like to do, ma'am."

"Do you mean that you'd rather not take me to Chessboard?"

"I can think of easier things," he said wryly.

Her eyes hardened. "Will I be such a burden?"

Morgan Chance eased into their talk. "Now, Kate. Amos here is doing me a favor."

She rounded on him. "Is it something you can't do?"

"Frankly, yes."

She regarded him, frowning. "I don't believe I understand."

"There are men who'd rather not see you get to Chessboard, Kate. Might as well face it."

"Because of you?"

"You might say that."

She opened her lips, then closed them. Then she murmured, "I should have had Peter meet me. I could have gone farther by train. I only stopped off here to see you, Morgan, to say hello, as you asked."

"They'd have stopped the train, taken you off it. Then nobody would ever see you again."

Carty could tell she had been startled. She leaned forward, watching her brother intently. "These men are your enemies, of course. They're trying to strike at you through me."

"You get the picture."

Her eyes slid sideways to touch Carty. "You must be very good at whatever it is you're good at, if my brother thinks you can do what he and these men can't."

"Good enough."

She still watched him—as a chicken might watch the coyote sniffling at the henhouse fence, Carty thought.

"What can you do that my brother, with all these men, cannot?"

"Get you safe to Chessboard."

"That isn't what I meant."

Carty shrugged. How could he tell this woman of the long hours he had spent with the Kiowa boys, learning to trail, to hunt, to eat where there was no food, to drink where there was no water? How could he put into mere words the ache and the pain of trotting endless hours over sunbaked desert sands, on lava and rock? He had spent close to ten years with the Kiowas; he was considered one of them before his father had come back to take him away.

Morgan Chance said, "Look, Kate. He's your one hope. He doesn't do it, nobody can."

"Very well. I accept your decision. I have no other choice." Her eyes touched her brother. "I know you are doing this with my best interests in mind, Morgan."

"You want to marry Pete Macklin. Fine. He'll make you a good husband. I want to see you settled in life, Kate.

But because you happen to be my sister, certain men are going to try to interfere if they can. Carty here will make sure they don't."

Kate stood up and shook out her skirt. It was as if she were shaking away all connections with her brother and these unkempt men in this back-trail saloon, Carty told himself. Maybe he didn't blame her too much. He himself wasn't too happy with this outfit.

She walked out, and every eye watched.

Chance growled, "Let's have a drink."

Carty said, "I need soap and water more."

He went out the batwing doors, untied the grulla, and walked him down the dusty street toward the livery stable. An old man was sleeping in the late sunlight, chair tilted against the stable wall. Carty did not wake him.

He unsaddled the horse, put him in a stall, and filled the bin with oats. He rubbed him down with the blanket, then went and got a bucket of water.

For a few minutes, he stood in the stable doorway, staring around the town. Few men came to Stovepipe. It was far off the beaten trails; no one had any reason to come here except men like Morg Chance and his riders. He wondered what Kate Chance really thought about it.

He put his eyes on the tall pines that rimmed the mountain. They were a long ride from the Chessboard. Their trail would run through barren country, among high peaks and canyons. They would go through Kiowa country, some Comanche. And there would be white men waiting for them. Killers.

Amos Carty shifted his gunbelt. When it came to killing, he would take a back seat to no man, if the life of Kate Chance depended on it. His own too, for that matter.

He went to the false-fronted building that was named

the Stovepipe Hotel. Another old man was behind the counter, also dozing. Carty rapped on the counter, and the man opened sleep-dimmed eyes.

"You want a room?"

"And water, and soap."

"You must've seen Miss Kate."

Carty took the key the man handed him, picked up his bedroll and saddlebags, and moved up the creaky stairs. The old man followed after a time, a kettle of hot water in one hand, a kettle of cold in the other.

Carty washed and shaved.

The grimy mirror showed him a lean face, dark brown by overmuch exposure to hot sunlight. His high cheekbones gave him something of the look of an Indian. Had his hair been black instead of tawny, and his eyes ebony instead of blue, he might have passed as one.

He was slightly under six feet tall, with broad, muscular shoulders and arms that bulged his buckskin jacket. His middle was lean, his legs were straight, unlike those of most men who spent long hours in the saddle. There was the suggestion of latent power in Amos Carty, as there might be in a sleeping puma.

Carty kicked off his boots, dropped his shellbelt, and lay down on the bed, locking his hands behind his head. The ceiling at which he stared was fly-specked and grimy, but he did not notice. His mind was far away, riding the dusty slopes, the fields of grama grass, the desert sands where the ocotillo and the cactus bloomed. Over most of the country through which they would ride he had already gone, in one year or another. He made his plans, slowly, carefully.

Much depended on the horses Morgan Chance would give him. He had no doubts about the grulla. It was strong and fleet, with endurance that had yet to be tested.

Kate Chance would be well mounted; he would insist on that. And the pack horses must be almost as good.

The air was filled with the aroma of cooking steak as he came down the stairs. Morgan Chance was waiting with Kate in the dusty lobby. They must have been quarreling; Kate was staring off into nowhere, and her brother was honestly scowling.

"We waited for you, Amos," Morg said grumpily.

Carty studied Kate Chance. "I'd rather eat alone."

Her eyes flashed at him. "I've been sitting here waiting for you, Mr. Carty. Had I known you were going to refuse Morgan's invitation, I'd have been eating by now."

Something had rubbed her raw. Or maybe she was always like this, the chip visible on her shoulder. Carty glanced at Morg. "Sorry," he said quietly.

Chance gestured with a hand. "Thought you'd want to talk over things."

"Nothing to talk about, except horses and grub. The horses got to be good, Morg. The grub doesn't matter so much."

Morgan Chance chuckled, and nudged his sister with a hand to her shoulder. "The Indian can live off the land, unlike most of us."

Her interest quickened. "Are you an Indian?"

His headshake was casual. Let her brother tell her about him and his early years. There was always a disinclination to talk in Amos Carty, and this woman didn't figure to change him.

With a nod, he brushed past them, went to the dining room, and found a table close to a window. The men glanced at him; one or two nodded, and the rest stayed bent above their plates.

To his surprise, the steak was cooked perfectly, the potatoes browned crisply. And the homemade biscuits just about melted in his mouth. He ate with concentration, knowing this might be the last really good meal he would eat in a long time. When he was done he walked to the big granite coffee pot and poured himself more coffee. He brought it back to his table and sipped it, smoking as he thought.

When he was done he walked across the room and stood at the table where Morgan Chance and his sister sat. They glanced up at him.

"We go at dawn," Carty said.

Kate said, "Dawn comes here a little before five, Mr. Carty."

He nodded, then put his eyes on her brother. "A good horse for her, Morg. Real good. And good ones for the packs."

He turned and walked away. She spoke softly, but he overheard her.

"I don't like that man, Morgan."

Carty did not smile. He was Indian-trained, he rarely showed his emotions; he never did, when he did not want to. He was not surprised that Kate Chance looked down her nose at him. He might have done the same, had he been an eastern-raised girl.

What was he, after all? A saddle bum with a fast hand for his gun, a nobody who wandered the back trails from Eagle Pass northward to the Milk River country. He made his way by punching cows or by hiring out his gun to some rancher having trouble with rustlers or a neighboring ranch. The wind stirred the dirt over which he had ridden; he had left no mark upon the land to mark the way of his going.

No reason for a girl to cotton to him.

It made no difference; he was taking her into Arizona to pay off a debt that Ken Stevens owed. By doing so, he was saving his life. The slate would be clean between himself and Morgan Chance then.

He thought about Ken Stevens as he walked down the single street beneath the stars in the darkened sky, savoring the cool wind laden with the smell of pine. He had known Ken Stevens, had ridden with him along the high trails, had worked with him on ranches here and there. Once Stevens had saved his life by warning him that two men were waiting in ambush for him. He felt he owed Ken one for that. Now he was paying it off, wiping that slate clean, too.

Carty built a cigarette, scratched a match on his Levi's, and lighted up. He savored the smoke, cupping the glowing end in his palm so it should not be seen. All his life he had been careful like that; it had been a trait Buffalo Horn had taught him.

He would have to be careful with that woman. She didn't have those habits. He frowned, thinking about that. Like as not, she would get them both killed, no matter what he did.

He hunkered down and rubbed out the quirley on the ground. He started to put the dead butt in his pocket, then grinned. No need to hide his sign in Stovepipe. He tossed the paper and shreds of tobacco high and watched the wind carry them off.

He swung about and walked back along the street.

CHAPTER 2

Carty was up before dawn, out of the hotel, and saddling the grulla when a candle was lighted in a hotel window. Two other windows glowed. He and Kate would have company for breakfast.

Morgan Chance and his sister were at the same table they had sat at last night. Hobe Talbert and Pike Shattuck were at another. Carty ignored them all to sit by himself. He ate ham and eggs, and pancakes dripping with syrup.

Out of the corners of his eyes, he saw that Kate Chance ate little or nothing. Just hot coffee. He felt an irritation deep inside him, but he finished his breakfast before he went to stand at their table.

"You eat," he told her.

She tilted her chin at him. "Are you giving me orders, Mr. Carty?"

"You eat. I'm not fixing to stop for lunch if you get hungry. This is no picnic."

She gasped and opened her mouth to reply, but by that time he was halfway across the room and going out the door. Pike and Hobe had lifted their heads, stared, and listened. They were grinning at each other now, he'd bet. Neither one of them would have dared to talk that way to Kate Chance. Only reason he did was because he was staking his life on this trip they were going to take.

The odds were bad enough without her adding to them.

He waited in the street, as patiently as any Apache. The day was going to be a good one, with plenty of sun. Maybe too much sun. He examined his Spencer rifle that was a seven-shot repeater and thrust it back into the scabbard. He knew his handgun as he did his face; it was always clean, always ready for his use.

Pike Shattuck walked up leading a bay mare that danced nervously at his tug. Hobe Talbert was slightly behind him with the pack horses, a roan and a pinto that looked like an Indian pony. The packs were already on, strapped down tightly.

The Chances came out of the hotel, side by side. Kate was scowling, but Morg had a big grin on his face. Carty knew without being told that she had been yammering away about him. Morg was probably right glad to be shet of her, maybe even pleased that Carty was able to stand up to her.

She gave him a cold look as she moved toward her bay. Morg came over and stood with him.

"How long you figure it will take, Amos?"

"Two, three weeks. Depends."

Chance rubbed his unshaven jaw. "If Kate gives you trouble—"

"She won't."

"She's not a peaceable woman, Indian."

"Morg, I'll get her through if I have to tie and gag her."

He said it loud enough for her to hear. Hobe and Pike were grinning fit to kill, behind her so she wouldn't see them. Kate turned and looked hard at him.

"Mr. Carty! I understand that we are going on a very dangerous trip. You may rest assured I will cause no trouble. I will do whatever you tell me."

He eyed her cold face. "You eat anything?"

Morg guffawed, and Carty could have kicked him.

Kate flushed slightly and said, "Two soft-boiled eggs. Does that please you?"

He nodded, swung into the kak, and reached for the trail ropes that were fastened to the pack horses' bridles. He moved out then, walking the grulla. His ears told him that Kate Chance was coming after him, walking the bay to the grulla's steps.

"So long, Kate, Carty. Luck!"

He turned, waved an arm, then set his eyes to the trail. It was going to be hot down on the flatlands. He hoped Kate Chance would be able to stand up to it.

He put the grulla to a lope when they came down out of the hills, the pack horses followed easily enough, and Kate Chance as well. The heat built up during the morning hours, but he kept the same pace, making good time while he could.

By early afternoon, it was time to water the horses. There was a sink a couple of miles off to one side—it was a Kiowa watering place on their war-party rides into Osage country. He had visited it with such a war party, before his father had taken him home. He had been sixteen then, big for his age and hard as a hickory knot.

He had been brown as a nut or any Indian, and he had smeared war paint on lavishly. Carty brooded, remembering. Two Osages had fallen before him in that rush on an unsuspecting village; he had run off three good horses he had given to Buffalo Horn.

There was water in the sink, as he had known there would be. He swung down and walked about, bent over, trying to find a sign. There was none. Nobody had used this hole for a long time.

He had not been looking for an Indian sign, but for any

evidence that white men had been here. He turned from the ground and saw Kate sitting in her saddle.

"Better walk a little," he advised.

"I am not at all tired."

He eyed her and shrugged. Her legs would be like boards come nightfall. It was her funeral. His job was to get her to Chessboard, not wet-nurse her. Still, she was a woman. Eastern, at that.

"You will be," he said flatly.

She eyed him coldly, turned her head, and looked back the way they had come. Carty sighed.

"Come tomorrow, you may not be able to ride."

She brought her head around to look at him. "I will ride, Mr. Carty."

He walked the grulla through the rocks, down a narrow trail, and onto the flatlands. It was the springtime of the year, the grass was thick, the white primroses and lavender verbenas were in bloom. Blue sageflowers nodded as they passed, and off to the south, he could make out the white petals of some prairie larkspur. It was beautiful country, or so Carty had always thought.

This was land that was hard on a man until he learned its ways. But the beauty all around him was reward enough for being here, if a man had eyes to see it.

All that afternoon they rode at the same ground-covering lope. The grulla raised no sweat, nor did the pack horses. His glance went over the bay, which seemed strong enough. One thing he gave Morg Chance: He knew horses.

It was dusk before he drew rein in a sheltered area, where a few trees grew, where there was grass for the horses. He sat the kak and watched Kate Chance swing down to the ground. She was stiff and sore, and he did not blame her, but she had asked for it.

She sank down on a rock and stared at her booted feet.

He hobbled the horses, removing the packs and saddles, and wiped them off with their saddle blankets, which he stretched out on the ground to dry. He sank to the ground, pulled off his boots, and drew on a pair of moccasins. He went to his rifle scabbard and lifted free the Spencer.

"You sit there," he told her. "I'll be back."

He went through the trees at a trot and began to climb into the rocks that bordered the little grove. Up this high he could see over a lot of country.

He sat there for half and hour, watching the flight of a bird in the sky, checking the ground for puffs of dust that might indicate where men were riding. There was no sign of a fire. Reassured, he came back to the girl and began to unpack their food.

He made a fire with sticks pointing outward like the spokes of a wagon wheel, cooked beans in a pot, and fried bacon. He mixed flour with some water from his big canteen, fashioning biscuits. When he was finished, he called the girl.

She lifted her head and stared at him. After a moment she rose to her feet and came toward him, walking with slow steps. There was pain in her, he knew. And a desperate tiredness.

He filled a plate and handed it over. She ate as if she could just manage to lift the fork to her lips. Carty fought back a smile. Might be best to stop over here a day or two, give her a chance to ease those muscles.

He thought about that as he chewed, then decided against it. They had a far trail to ride; the sooner they got to Chessboard, the sooner he'd be rid of her. Before she was done eating he pulled a quilted blanket from her saddleroll and placed it on the ground.

They drank the coffee they had made, but her eyes were closing. She looked at that blanket hungrily, so he said, "Take it back under the trees and roll up."

She did not argue, but did what he said.

Carty put dirt on the fire and redded up by starlight. When the fire was out he took his own roll and walked with it about fifty feet from where the fire had been. He stretched out, his Spencer close at hand, and closed his eyes.

If anybody came riding up, the grulla would let him know.

A wind sprang up, lulling him to sleep as it sifted through the ocotillo stalks.

CHAPTER 3

The wind was still blowing when they crossed White River two days later and edged their way closer to the Llano Estacado. By this time, Kate Chance was sitting easier in the saddle, some of the soreness gone out of her, and Carty noticed she was giving him curious glances.

She had not spoken more than a dozen words to him.

"You're not a talkative man," she said now.

"Sound travels."

She looked around them at the empty plain. "There isn't anyone around that I can see."

"Gets to be a habit."

Kate Chance frowned. "If you want me to be quiet, just say so."

"Makes no difference to me."

"I've been watching you. We've been riding out in clear view of anyone who wanted to see us. I thought you were so good at hiding yourself."

He caught the mockery in her voice. Stung, he said coldly, "Nobody around to see us. Or follow us."

"How can you tell?"

"Been looking at our back trail. No dust. None. Been watching the birds, too. Nothing to startle them. Nobody around."

Kate thought about that, turning what he had said over in her mind. She protested, "My brother expected us to have trouble."

"Hasn't come yet. It will."

She squirmed in her saddle. "You're the most irritating man I've ever known. Do you always talk in just a couple of words?"

"You savvy my drift, don't you?"

She ignored him after that, to bend her head against the wind. It seemed to Kate Chance that it had been blowing like this for days. Twice in the past hour she had almost lost her hat, and not until Carty had told her to tie a long ribbon around it had she felt certain that it would not blow away.

"Is it always like this, so windy?"

"Sometimes she gusts a mite. The Kiowas call it the *ka goum' gia*, the wild wind. But it's a help."

"A help?" She could hardly catch her breath.

"Blows the grass so we don't leave tracks."

She looked behind her and saw the grasses fitfully moving one way and then another as the winds swirled and changed directions. Whatever marks their horses' hooves had left behind them would soon be gone.

Unconsciously, she rode closer to him and studied him through wind-narrowed eyes. He was a strong man—she could see the muscles shift as he moved his body—and reliant. There was something about him that inspired confidence—the way he rode, the manner of his seat in the kak, perhaps. Always ready.

Yes, that was it. There was no ease in him, he was like a wild animal. What was that her brother had called him? Indian.

"Are you an Indian?" she asked.

He gave her a sideways glance, and she thought his eyes were cold.

"I was raised by Kiowas. My father was a mountain man, then an Army scout. He knew the Kiowas, lived with them a spell. When the war broke out he had to have some place to put me. I grew up with the Kiowas, even went on war parties with them."

He sensed the horror in her.

"D-did you take scalps?"

"I was a Kiowa. Didn't know any better."

"And now?"

"I gave up scalping some time back."

He heard her indrawn breath and would have smiled if he had been a smiling man. Well, maybe he had gotten her off his back for a time. She fell away and rode behind him, in back of the pack horses.

He camped that night in the lee of some hills that ran their bulk close to the Canadian. It was a grassy spot he picked, sheltered by pines and boulders. Before he unpacked the horses or unsaddled he put on his moccasins and went off by himself up into the hills, as he always did.

Carty came back an hour later, his face calm.

Kate asked, "Did you see anything?"

"Just grass and water and some trees."

She watched as he began to prepare the food. On impulse she rose and went to him. "Let me do that. I'm tired of your cooking."

He stepped back and watched her. He was a man used to doing his own cooking. To him food was a necessity. There were only rare moments in his life, excepting always his years with the Kiowas, when he ate woman-cooked grub.

Yet there was a difference, he realized, as soon as he put the first mouthful between his teeth. She had found some herbs and added them, and made some sort of sauce with flour and water and those herbs that was mighty flavorful.

Her coffee was better than his, too.

He built a cigarette in the peace and quiet of the evening, sipping his coffee and staring off across the plain. He felt relaxed, at ease with the world.

There had been no sign of any enemies, so far. Could be he had missed them, coming this far north. He would have to strike south in a day or two, though, to get to Chessboard, and it might be that Nogales Jack or Rawhide Bledsoe would cut across their trail.

Time to worry about that when it happened.

The girl said, "This is very empty country, isn't it?"

"Way we been traveling, yes. We skirted Fort Cobb and Tascosa. No sense in letting ourselves be seen."

"There was a fort? A town?"

"Just out of sight. If we couldn't see them, they couldn't see us."

Kate stared. "You've been making me sleep out on the ground, when I could have been in a bed?"

"Too dangerous."

"You certainly are cautious."

"You want to live?"

She could not believe there were men who would harm her, not even out in this wild country. Indians, yes. But not white men. She spoke out about this, rather tartly.

"Most men won't. It's a sort of code. Some will. Men like Nogales Jack and Rawhide . . ."

His shrug was eloquent.

"They have nothing against me."

"Against your brother."

Kate thought about that. She shifted uncomfortably.

"He's a lot older than I am. Actually, he's only my half brother. His mother is my mother. We had different fathers. He was always a headstrong boy, Morgan was. He took to riding off by himself when he was sixteen. I think he got into trouble."

Carty could have told her he had, and the manner of it. Morg Chance was not a pleasant man, not when there was money to be had for the taking, and he had few compunctions about his way of making it his own. There had been stories Carty had heard in the towns or around the lonely campfires. He had listened but said nothing. What Morg Chance did was no concern of his.

"My mother insisted I be sent East," she went on, poking at the fire with a stick. "I grew away from Morgan. Only when I met Peter Macklin and became engaged, I decided to write Morgan about it."

That had been a mistake, Carty thought.

"He insisted I come to see him." Her eyes lifted, and met his across the little fire. "That was the first time I knew he was in trouble."

"Doesn't make sense," he muttered.

"What doesn't?"

"Why he should bring you into it. No need to, was there?"

"He said he wanted to see me, that it had been a long time since we had seen each other."

Morg Chance hadn't struck him as a man who would go to any lengths just to run eyes over a sister he hadn't seen for ten or fifteen years. There was more to it than that. Carty let his mind savor the problem as he put out the fire and watched the girl carry her gear fifty feet away into the darkness beneath a tree.

Carty had something to do with it—he sensed this as he might sense an enemy coming up on him in the darkness. But what connection he might have with whatever it was, was beyond him. He unrolled his blankets and lay down, drawing the blanket over him. For a long time he lay staring up at the stars, thinking.

The next day they cut straight west and in time came to a vast stretch of hoofbeaten ground running north and south. Kate was surprised by it. He could see her, out of the corners of his eyes, staring at it.

"Goodnight-Loving cattle trail," he told her.

"But why are we taking it?" she asked as he turned their horses southward toward the distant Llano Estacado.

His arm lifted, pointing. Far to the southward she could see a dust haze. "Cattle coming. Thousand head or more. Whatever trail we leave will be soon gone under those hooves."

He rode until they could almost see the cattle. Then using some rock ridges as a shelter, he turned to the west. Now as he rode, he dragged a blanket behind him at the end of a rope, and he trailed Kate and the pack horses that way for mile after mile.

"Blanket rubs out the tracks," he muttered when she asked him. "Wouldn't fool a 'Pache, but Nogales Jack and Bledsoe are town men."

They moved across sandy soil here, and where he could, Carty took advantage of tumbled rocks and an occasional wash, riding down into it and moving along with its steep banks on either side to hide them. He was not concerned so much with making time as he was in hiding his trail and themselves.

As they came out of cottonwoods beside a stream where they had stopped to water their horses and refill canteens, a tiny puff of distant dust caught Carty's eyes. He reined in, signaling Kate to stop. From the scabbard under his right leg he lifted out the Spencer and held it across his hip.

"What is it?"

"Someone coming. Get back under the trees."

"I don't see anyone."

"They're there, just the same."

His hand swung the grulla around and he moved, drawing the pack horses after him, following the girl in under the trees. They made no sound, except when one of the pack horses snorted, but waited quietly, staring westward. The gurgling of the little stream made a soft sound, which blended with the wind that stirred the leaves.

There were half a dozen riders; Carty could make out that much after a time, and they moved in single file. He slid the rifle into the scabbard. Kate stared at him.

"It's safe enough. Come along."

He moved from the cottonwoods out across the dusty soil, bringing the pack horses with him. Kate came at his heels, swaying in the saddle, frowning.

Turning in the saddle, he said, "They're Kiowa-Apache. Relatives, sort of. Be easy."

He toed the grulla to a trot. Instantly the six riders broke apart, swinging wide. Carty raised his right hand and swung it outward, making the sign for friend. The grulla picked up speed and began to canter.

"*A'kou*," he called.

They were short men, deep-chested and with powerful arms and legs. They wore silver hairplates, and the trappings of their horses were ornamented with silver pieces. All carried rifles, and two had bows and quivers of arrows strapped to their backs.

"I see you, Spotted Dog," Carty smiled.

An older man grunted, leaning forward slightly the better to scan this white man who spoke his language as though born to it. There was neither friendliness nor enmity in his hard black eyes.

"Who knows Spotted Dog so well he can speak his name?"

"The man who saved his life against the Utes during the fight in which Setoyote was killed."

The older man straightened and seemed almost to shake himself. The wind blew his long hair across his face, but he did not move a hand to brush it away. His black eyes seemed almost to burn through that dark, black hair.

"I fought with no white man beside me that day."

"I am Kue-tae, the White Wolf."

"Huh!"

The others were closer now, grinning and nodding their heads as Spotted Dog threw back his head and laughed. He urged his pony closer to Carty, threw his arms about him, and was embraced in turn.

A little behind them, Kate Chance stared in something like shock. She had always believed that Indians were a solemn, morose people, but to see them laughing and patting this man who rode with her, all of them speaking at once like ladies at a sewing bee, vaguely disturbed her.

She listened to their talk but could make no sense of it, though she grew aware, after a while, that they must have been speaking of her, because from time to time their eyes slid away from Carty to take her in. There was hoarse laughter; of the sort men make when they are being crude, she decided.

They talked for some time, and now they were serious. Her attention wandered; she stared outward across the stretch of land to the west, seeing the blue sky overhead run down to meet a range of hills in the distance. She knew they were in the New Mexico Territory, but she did not know how far they had yet to go to reach Arizona. They had been on the trail for five days now; they still had far to travel.

A sudden quiet made her glance up.

Carty was sitting his saddle, looking at her. The Kiowa-Apaches were half a mile away and traveling at a canter.

"You through dreaming, we'll get along."

"I was just wondering how much longer we had to be together," she announced coldly.

"Another week. We can make some good time now. Nobody around."

"How do you know—oh. I suppose those friends of yours told you."

"They've come from Brazos country, where they were visiting some relations. No white men around."

They made good time across the flatlands, but they were coming into mountainous country now, where juniper and firs made their stand. Carty angled their trail upward in among boulders and tumbled rocks, where white spruce rubbed branches with the ponderosa pines. The wind was colder here, with a biting edge that made the girl shiver. There were the lower edges of the Rockies where they formed part of the continental divide, watered by countless little streams of water that fed into the Rio Grande.

Carty made his camp up high, before a huge boulder that towered above his head and made good shelter from the wind. He could see a far piece from here, out across the valley all the way to Taos. He made a small fire over which would be cooked three fish he had caught in one of the streams through which they had waded the horses.

Kate did the cooking. He had learned to let her handle that chore. She always flavored it with herbs and suchlike that she saw along the way and he got for her, carrying them in a doeskin parfleche bag that had been a gift, long ago, from old Buffalo Horn's wife.

He said, when they were eating, "We head southwest tomorrow, into warmer country."

She ignored that to ask, "What did those Indians say?"

"We mostly talked about their back trail."

She frowned. "That wouldn't make them laugh the way they did."

"Oh, that. Told them you were my squaw."

"Your *squaw?*"

"Wife, then."

She was so indignant she was speechless. He saw it and smiled faintly. "Wouldn't want me to tell them your brother was too scared to fetch you here himself, would you?"

"You think Morg was scared to do this?"

He eyed her coolly. "Don't you?"

"I don't think he's afraid of anything."

Carty shrugged. He knew the girl was studying him from under lowered brows, that there was a coldness in her to match the mountain wind itself. He paid her no mind. He was too intent on what he had to do.

With handfuls of dirt he began covering the fire, at which the girl protested. "It's going to be freezing tonight! Why don't you leave that fire so we can sleep beside it?"

"Get back under the rock. Nobody can see the rock from the valley. A blind man could spot a fire in this darkness."

"They may have already seen it if they're looking for it."

He nodded. "It's what I'm hoping."

She gasped. "You *want* them to find us?"

"If they come after me in the dark, the advantage is mine."

The fire was out. The darkness came in around them like a sheltering mantle, she realized. She could make him out, but barely.

"How can you see them?"

"Won't have to. I'll hear them."

She shook her head, but rose and walked back under the overhang where he was busy making a bed out of tree boughs and dirt. He spread her bedroll, and taking up his rifle, he moved off into the night. Kate Chance listened, but she could not hear his footfalls; he moved like a wild animal in those moccasins he had put on after dismounting.

Carty made his climb up onto the big boulder, sliding across its top so as not to skyline himself against the stars. He had not expected trouble until now, but he had been prepared for it. Any trouble that would come, he felt certain, would take place from now on. Might be this night. Nogales Jack and Rawhide Bledsoe could be out there waiting.

They were town men. Nogales Jack was a gambler more used to the felt top of a gaming table than to a hard-ground bed. Bledsoe was a hanger-on, a drifter, a man with a fast gun who hired out where some man had a need of it. They might hire other men, and probably would. Certainly one of them would be a tracker.

It was the tracker he had to be wary of; no telling what a man like that would know. Best to be on the safe side.

He slept after a time, dozing lightly, as he had trained himself to do. The slightest sound would wake him, the rattle of an overturned pebble, even the brush of cloth against a bush. Twice he woke to slide back and forth across the rock and listen, but only the familiar night sounds came to his ears.

In the morning, after a breakfast of bacon and biscuits, they went down off the mountainside into Chaco River country. Carty rode carefully here, his Spencer across his saddlehorn. The mountains, with their places of concealment, were things of the past: he was heading onto level plains, with only an occasional mountain lifting its peak upward like an island in a grassy sea.

They made good time; Carty did not want to stop in the open to eat or rest. Spotted Dog had told him where he would find water; he had no worry about that. But he was uneasy, with an animal restlessness that came upon him occasionally and was usually followed by trouble.

When they came to a stretch of grama grass that ran up onto the slope of a mesa, Carty headed toward it. In among the tumbled rocks at its base he found an open space, covered over with grass and protected from view by the talus.

"You get in there and stay put," he told Kate. "Keep the horses with you. Don't show yourself, on no account."

"And what are you going to do?"

"Get water, scout around."

She opened her mouth to argue but he rode off, not wanting to listen to her voice but to be by himself, to open up his senses to this feeling of unease that shared the kak with him. His rifle was in his hand as the grulla horse ran, and he was always turning in the saddle, staring around him, to the front and then along his back trail.

He saw nothing. The rocks that hid Kate Chance were like a stone curtain, and beyond them the flat was empty. Still, that feeling persisted.

When he came to the rocky ridge behind which there was a basin of water, he paused. The back of his neck prickled, and he moved his shoulders—half to relieve the feeling, half in irritation at himself. His eyes studied the ridge.

It was a good climb, but the grulla could make it. His eyes fell to the trail itself. Yes, the horse could go up it, but with his ironshod hooves, he would make a lot of noise.

Carty dismounted, took off his boots, and slipped into his Kiowa moccasins. Taking his rifle in hand and flinging the canteens over a shoulder, he moved up the sloping rock, avoiding the telltale pebbles on the path.

He stepped around a corner of rock and froze.

Two men were hunkered down at the waterhole, staring off into space. They wore faded red shirts and chaps; their guns hung low in worn leather holsters. Each man had his hat on the back of his head, and one man was chewing a weed stalk.

"You waitin' for anyone?" Carty asked.

They moved sideways, their hands going to their guns. But the Spencer was aimed between them, and the sound of its cocking was loud. Their hands fell away from their guns, and one of them grinned shamefacedly.

"Took us by surprise, mister."

"Sure did." He put his eyes around the sink, seeing only the men and no sign of any others. Where were their horses?

"No need to be riled," the bigger man said.

"Turn around, both of you."

"Now, look," the smaller man began. His eyes were black and hard; there was a cruelty stamped on his thin face. He appeared to hesitate, then said coldly, "We got nothing to do with you."

At a venture, Carty asked, "How's Nogales these days?"

The smaller man did not move a muscle, but the big man opened his eyes wide, blurting out, "You know Jack?"

"Shut your lip," snarled the other.

The Spencer rose, then moved slightly. "Turn. Now!"

The smaller man sneered, but he turned his back, slowly and with a hard look at Carty. The bigger man followed his example. Then, at Carty's command, their hands went to the buckles of their shellbelts. Moments later they were at their feet.

"Up against the far wall, boys."

"You goin' to let him get away with this, Lou?"

"I'm a patient man, Charley."

When their palms were flat against the huge rocks, Carty bent and filled the canteens. He lifted the big Bentley that was propped against a rock, shook it to judge the amount of water it held, then filled that, too.

"I'm taking your guns and your canteen," Carty told them.

The man known as Lou snarled, "You won't get away with this. We'll follow your tracks. We'll catch up to you."

Carty nodded. For two men to be set afoot in this country was a bad thing. They had not reacted the way he thought they might; this meant there were others around on whom they could call for help. Their horses might be around, they could be with those others. At any rate, he knew they would not be here, alone and helpless, for very long.

He backed away silently, then turned and ran.

He had seen no sign of any rifles. They might be on their saddles, but he had no time to go hunting their mounts. He had to ride back to Kate Chance and get her away from here, the sooner the better for both of them.

Carty picked up his boots and carried them in a hand as he swung into the kak and put the grulla to a fast run. He wanted distance between himself and those men, who had been left at the waterhole to gun him down.

But no. Wait. The men who wanted Kate Chance had no way of knowing that Amos Carty was bringing that girl alone through the New Mexico Territory. They were not here to swap bullets with him. Then why? To set up an alarm if Morgan Chance should come riding with his sister, backed by a dozen gunmen?

That made no sense either. Men like Nogales Jack and Rawhide Bledsoe would never leave only two men to try to stop a dozen.

He turned in the saddle, staring back. A thin plume of smoke was rising from the rock ridge. They had split up their forces in an attempt to find out which trail Morgan Chance would be following. Two men were here, more would be at the next watering place, others would be scattered across the countryside. That smoke would bring them all on the run.

Carty snarled. A wolf might snarl like that, deprived of food it conceived to be its own. He should have gut-shot both those men. He would have, years back when he had been a Kiowa. A dead enemy is a safe enemy. He was half minded to go back, toss those men their handguns, and have it out with them.

If he had been alone . . .

He had the girl to consider. Her safety was the important thing. He stretched the grulla into an all-out run, heading it for the mesa. He had intended to throw away the shellbelts with the Colts still in their holsters, but now he thought better of it. Those extra guns and that ammunition might come in right handy.

He came around the edge of the tumbled rocks and yanked the grulla to a sliding halt. The pack horses were here, browsing contentedly. But there was no sign of Kate Chance, nor of her bay mare.

CHAPTER 4

Morgan Chance came out of the saloon and stood blink-
ing in the noonday sunlight. He was at peace with his
world. His sister was off to Arizona with Amos Carty, and
in another few days he would follow.

He grinned. Kate did not know he was going to come
after her; she had no idea of what he had in mind. She
would have screamed blue murder if she could have
guessed. His grin stretched a little farther, thinking of
what she might have said.

She would say it in time, of course, when he made his
play. But by then he would have what he wanted, she
would have no way to gainsay him, and he, Morgan
Chance, would be a power in the land. He thought about
that, relishing the idea.

He had ridden the long trails for too long a time. He
was getting on in years, in his late thirties. Not old, no,
but he had lost that first bright sheen of youth where all
things can be accomplished, where opportunity is waiting
for that knock to throw wide its door.

Morg Chance was tired of being an outlaw.

He wanted respectability, a good name. It was all there
for the taking, the good name, the wealth his soul
craved, the power. Just stretch out his hand and wrap his
fingers around it. His sister was helping him, so was Amos
Carty, though neither of them knew it.

He blinked against the early-morning sunlight tipping

the peaks of the Horseheads with scarlet fire, building a cigarette and smiling to his thoughts. The Indian would get Kate to Chessboard. That was the first step in his plan. After that, well—then Amos Carty had to leave.

An uneasy chill ran down his spine. He did not exactly fear Carty, but he was wary of him. He had seen him draw once, in a dusty Texas town, against two men. His gunhand had not seemed to move, but the iron had bucked twice in his grip, and those two men were dead.

It had seemed so easy, as though Carty had not even tried. He pointed his Colt, and that was that. He may have had no Injun blood in him, but he had the stoicism of the red man. His face had not lost its cold, hard look. He had been as impassive as ever.

The two men needed killing. No doubt of that. It was the way Carty had gone about it, as though he had a job to do and wanted to get it over and done with as fast as possible.

A boot sounded on the porch plankings. He turned and saw Pike Shattuck yawning as he came up beside him.

"I'm gettin' tired of this place, Morg. When we moving out?"

"Soon, now. Tomorrow or the next day."

"How far you think that Carty is?"

"Into New Mexico, pretty far. Not into Arizona. Not yet."

Shattuck looked hard at him. "You thinkin' about Nogales Jack and that other one? They may miss Carty and your sister. They might not miss us."

Chance shrugged. "They make their try, we'll be ready for it. But we're cutting north toward Dodge City and the Arkansas. We'll follow the Gunnison for a time, then swing down by the way of the Colorado."

Shattuck grunted. "Seems a long way around."

"Long but safe."

"There is that. I'm hungry. You comin' in?"

"In a minute."

He wanted more time to stand here and breathe the crisp air, to savor what lay ahead of him. His was a foolproof plan; it could not fail of success. Only Carty could make trouble, and he did not think that was likely. By the time he himself got to Chessboard, the Indian would be long gone.

No, he was safe enough. Kate would cause no trouble once he was there. It might be that her tongue would grow a little sharper, but he could put up with that. No female tongue ever spilled blood from a man—not without help, that is.

He smoked the cigarette down to its end, then tossed it into the street. Squinting up at the sun, he told himself it might be a good idea to ride out of here today, not wait until tomorrow. The boys were getting restless. Be a good idea to get them on the trail, keep them busy.

He turned and went into the boardinghouse, satisfaction ripe inside him. Wouldn't be too long now before he was a mighty important man.

Carty came out of the saddle and ran for the rocks as soon as he noticed that Kate was nowhere around. He hit the ground and rolled behind a chunk of sandstone, his iron in his hand.

There was only silence. One of the pack horses lifted its head to look at him, then began to nibble some more at the bunch grass. Carty waited as might a true Kiowa, but after a time, especially when he saw a chipmunk come out and sun himself on a nearby rock, he knew he was alone.

He stood, and the chipmunk fled.

Still in his moccasins, he walked around the little enclosure, studying the ground. There had been men here, strange men: He could see the marks of their boots. A smaller mark showed where Kate had tried to run, her toe-tracks deeper than the others.

They had caught her about here, made her mount up, had taken her with them. He had seen nothing to indicate that they had gone to the waterhole. They had traveled the other way, back toward the Brazos.

Mounting, he gathered up the pack horses and took off at a gallop, half leaning from the saddle, the better to see the hoofprints on the ground. After a little study, he knew there had been two men. Kate rode between them. They were not moving too swiftly; maybe they thought they were safe.

Carty gave the grulla its head. The mouse-colored horse was fast, but even more important, it had endurance. As he rode, he lifted out the Spencer and held it ready. He was going to get Kate back, one way or t'other.

Their trail was easy to read; they must have been town men. He wondered if they might be Nogales Jack and Rawhide Bledsoe. If he could come up on those two, he had a notion that there would be no more hunting for Kate Chance. The hired guns simply would not care enough.

They were headed for a rock outcropping that formed part of a ridge drifting upward into the high hills. Once there, they could turn and see him on these flats; a good rifleman could pick him off with no trouble at all. He circled the grulla, aimed at a distant knoll. If he stayed out of rifle range and got to that knoll, those two men would know they'd caught hold of a fight.

There were no shots at him. He did not expect any; shots would only pinpoint their position for him. He walked the horse between some rocks and dismounted, dropping the reins. The grulla would stay put, he could forget about it. On moccasined feet he slid between the rocks and began his climb, the Spencer in his hand.

He went at a run, bent over, racing past a clump of rabbit brush. There was no trail here. He made his way along the lower slopes, keeping always in what shadow there was, using rocks as barriers between himself and the men who would be watching for him.

They would not hurt Kate, not yet. Carty fancied they wanted her as a hostage to get their hands on Morg Chance; not that this would do them any good. He fancied that the outlaw would never offer himself up in exchange for his sister. They would kill her, he knew that, but only when they became convinced that Chance was not going to come where they wanted him.

He made good time, silent on the rawhide soles. He came up into the high ground, and now he knew he must be more careful. He had no idea where the men were hidden; he must hunt and search as he had done as a youngster, playing games with the Kiowa boys.

Now he was crawling on his belly, slowly so as not to make a sound. When his shellbelt made a scratching sound he put a hand to the buckle and eased it off, to carry it in his left hand. On elbows and knees he moved forward, eyes turning left and right and then behind him. He did not want to be surprised up here, not flat on his belly and facing the wrong way.

Movement to the left caught his eye, where a rock wren came streaking skyward. Something had startled that bird. Might be a bobcat, but he didn't think so. He swung around and moved swiftly yet quietly along the rocktop. When he came to a dip he slid down it and found himself on a narrow ledge.

The ledge brought him to a wide, flat rock that looked down onto a stretch of grass almost completely surrounded by rocky walls, a tiny island hidden from the view of anyone riding beyond this pile of rocks.

Kate Chance was down there, sitting on a flat stone, head hanging as though dejected. Two men were with her, busy gathering sticks and brush to make a fire. Neither of the men was Nogales Jack. He did not know what Bledsoe looked like. These were probably men hired to ride out with them who had stumbled on the place where he'd left Kate.

They had not seen him, so he shrank back against the rock wall, needing time to think. He must not let them start that fire, to draw more of their crowd toward him. There was no way down from this height toward that grass island; he had looked.

He moved to the ledge, rifle before him.

"You down there."

They stiffened, hands filled with chunks of wood. Kate sprang to her feet, staring up at him.

"Stay put, you two. Kate, get your mare. And their horses, too. Walk them out of that opening nice and easy, then head east. I'll meet you."

He could not shoot those two down in cold blood. Once he might have, but no longer. Carty snarled in his throat. These men deserved death. If he had been down there with them, he would have given them a chance to go for their guns, but up here on the rockface, he thought it too much like murder.

He waited until Kate was in the saddle and was holding the reins of the other horses. He watched her leave, waited until he knew she would be well away. Then he slid behind a rock outcropping and padded back the way he had come.

Hoarse yells told him of their rage, but their rifles were in the scabbards on their horses, and those yells faded as he raced along. He must be there when Kate arrived with the horses. Having extra saddle mounts would help: They could change horses to make better time.

She was waiting when he came sliding down the slope. Her eyes seemed deep-sunk as she stared at him. Maybe now she knew the kind of men they were up against. He hoped so, anyhow.

Shoving the rifle into its boot, he mounted and turned the grulla.

"We got a run to make," he told her.

She said nothing, following him out onto the flatland. They went away from the rocks at a fast gallop, the pack horses and the saddle mounts behind them. Carty headed southward into Hosta Butte country. They would travel through Campbell's Pass and pick up the Zuni River. They had a far piece to travel. It would take them another three or four days before they were in Arizona Territory.

Toward late afternoon, they stopped to change horses. It was then that Kate said, "You aren't covering your tracks the way you did a few days ago."

"Best to move fast right now. It'll take time to get themselves together. Two of them don't have horses anymore. We'll keep on going until after nightfall."

They camped in a wash, where Carty made a small fire Indian fashion, with the dried squaw wood sticks pointing inward so that there was little smoke, and the walls of the wash would hide the flames. They ate swiftly, silently, and when they were done, Carty poured dirt on the fire and then walked up the bank to stretch out with his face to the east.

Behind him, Kate lay in her bedroll and stared up at

the stars. She had almost forgotten what it felt like to sleep in a civilized bed. It seemed to her that she had been traveling forever with this quiet man who was so much at home in this wild country.

She wondered if he meant to stay awake all night. She did not understand how he could do it. She was tired, so tired her eyelids felt like lead weights. She was warm in the bedroll, and comfortable enough, she guessed, though sheets and a proper mattress would have been far better. She slept even as she was thinking this.

Alone in the night, Carty scanned the grasslands. His ears heard nothing, but from time to time he turned to glance at the grulla. The horse had even better hearing than he, and would be alert for danger.

He dozed and woke a dozen times as the stars rolled in the heavens.

At dawn he was up and making a fresh fire, cooking the few slabs of bacon he was allotting to them. He was busy at this when Kate came to crouch beside him, taking the coffee pot and pouring water from a canteen into it, and then ground coffee beans.

As they ate, the world gew lighter. There were dark clouds to the north, and Carty studied them as he sipped his coffee. They looked like rainclouds to him, and rain would be appreciated right about now. Help to cover their tracks. He did not think it would rain, though; it rarely rained in New Mexico Territory.

They would make Campbell's Pass by nightfall, with luck. The next day they would be in Arizona Territory. He kicked dirt on the fire and watched as Kate stored the coffee pot and the skillet. She was pretty handy at woman's work; she went about things with no waste motion.

She turned once, sensing he was watching her.

"Yes? Is there something you wanted?"

"Ought to be at Chessboard in two more days. Then you'll be shet of me."

She smiled faintly. "My brother and I owe you a lot for what you're doing."

"Just paying a debt."

Her eyebrows rose. "A debt?"

"Man I know named Stevens said he would pay your brother some money Morg figured belonged to him. I told Morg I'd guarantee that payment. My friend went off, so I rode in to Stovepipe. My taking you to Chessboard will write off that debt my friend owed."

"You will be paid for doing this, Mr. Carty. Peter will see to that. You have my promise."

Carty shrugged. The money would be nice. He hadn't much more than half a dozen gold eagles in his jeans. He guessed she didn't realize he was doing this for himself, because he had given his word. Still, money would be nice.

They mounted up and rode out of the wash before the sun was fully over the Cebolleto Mountains, Kate in the lead and Carty bringing up the rear. He wanted a clear view of their back trail, and turned often in the kak to let his eyes move slowly over the grasslands.

The thunderheads caught up to them in the middle of the day, bringing rain and a chill dampness that penetrated the slicker Carty put on and the coat that Kate slipped into. The horses walked with heads down, tiredness in them as well as in the man and woman. Twice during the day they changed mounts. They ate no lunch, and Kate Chance was wondering whether or not they would eat at their night camp.

They went through the Zunis and moved down onto the flatlands by early evening, coming in sight of the river as dusk lay across the world. The rain had stopped, dripping from the leaves while they made a campfire in a grove of cottonwoods. They did not take long to eat. Carty was restless; his uneasiness was strong inside him. He rose often and moved to stare out along their back trail while Kate paused in her eating to watch him worriedly.

If Nogales Jack and Rawhide Bledsoe were going to hit them, they would have to do it soon—tonight, maybe, or sometime tomorrow. After that, they should be on Chessboard, where Kate Chance would be safe.

He had dozed a little in the saddle when he could, he was not as tired as he thought; he was too keyed up, he supposed. Tonight and tomorrow. After that he would be able to ride off, hopefully with hard cash in his jeans for a job well done.

He took the Spencer and moved into the darkness away from the trees, after dousing the fire. He could not see Kate behind him. She was in her blankets, close to the ground. There was nothing to give away their position.

He lay down himself, cradling the rifle across his arms. This low to the ground he could see any riders approaching—their bodies and that of their horses would be outlined against the stars. He was awake a long time before he fell asleep, thinking about the men who were following them.

They would know where he was bound, of course; they would have to hit them before they got to Chessboard. Might be they had decided to go on ahead, expecting to come between them and the ranch tomorrow. They might want daylight, to see. They had no fear of fighting by night, as some Indians did, but they wouldn't want to go shooting blindly for fear of hitting their own men.

He woke to the first gray paleness of an early dawn. He

looked around him a long time before he rose to his feet
and moved toward the cottonwoods. Kate was still asleep.
He let her lie as he built a small fire and put bacon into
the skillet.

He had watched her make coffee often enough to know
what she did, and he imitated her. The smell of frying
bacon and coffee would bring her out of that bedroll fast
enough.

She said as she came up beside him, tucking in a few
strands of her brown hair, "I'll be grateful when we get to
that ranch."

"Reckon."

"To sleep in a proper bed, to have warm water in which
to wash, is something I never really appreciated before,
Mr. Carty."

"I can count the times I slept in a bed."

She stared at him. "Are you joking?"

"No, ma'am. Raised by Kiowas like I was, bed was a lot
of brush with a skin draped over it. Even when my pa
came and took me away with him after the war, it wasn't
much better. Pa was a mountain man and Army scout; he
lived with the sky for a roof most of the time. He took me
with him on his hunts, and to live for a time in a little
cabin he built himself up in the Sweetwater country in
Wyoming Territory. Those were the times I slept in a
bed."

She accepted the biscuit and bacon he handed her,
frowning at him. "You could make a living at hunting?"

"Wasn't much of a living, but we managed. We shot
buffalo and trapped for fur. Made a dollar here and there.
Then Pa got himself killed by some Hunkpapa Sioux.
After that, well—I just drifted."

He wiped the bottom of the skillet with a chunk of biscuit, aware that she was staring at him.

"Surely you must have an occupation?"

He chuckled. "Punched cows for a time, went up the cattle trails to Dodge City and Abilene. Slept between sheets for the first time in my life at Dodge. Sure was a funny feeling."

"But how do you live?"

"Don't need much. Live off the land. Buy flour and bacon, bullets. Can get along all right for the rest of it."

"You never went to school?"

"Pa taught me how to read and write. Enough to get by. Man like me doesn't need any more."

She shook her head. "I have never met a man like you before, Mr. Carty."

"Don't reckon you have, but there's a lot of us wandering around. Men with fast gunhands who sell their guns to somebody who needs them."

"Have you?"

His eyes lifted; he stared at her. "It's easier than riding drag behind a lot of longhorns. I have, ma'am. And made good money at it. Some of it I even put into a bank."

He rose and walked toward the grulla, munching at the grass. He saddled the horse and the bay mare, put the pack saddles on the others, then saddled the extra mounts. He paused then and ran his eyes out across the land, seeing the mountains bulking behind him, and the sunlight flashing on the river to one side.

There was no movement, no sound other than the wind rustling the cottonwood leaves. He took the bedrolls from Kate, strapped them down with the piggin strings, then swung into the kak.

They followed the river southwestward at a steady canter. Toward noon they changed horses and went on for another hour when Carty reined in near a little stream, where there was good forage for the horses and a tumble of big rocks past which the water gurgled. He un-saddled and let them roll and drink from the brook.

Kate busied herself with the bacon and flour, making biscuits over the tiny fire Carty had fashioned. She said, "I'm getting tired of bacon and biscuits. It's a good thing the ranch isn't too far away."

"I'd shoot us an antelope if—"

She saw him tense and turn away. Seven men were coming up over a rise in the ground and holding their horses steadily in their direction. They were unkempt and dirty, they all had beards or chin stubble, and they were heavily armed. Kate rose to her feet, crying out softly.

Carty said, "Into the rocks. Don't run."

He came after her, the Spencer in his hand.

The riders held their course but began to split apart.

CHAPTER 5

As he followed the girl, Carty picked up the spare shell-belts and carried them with him. Lowering himself behind a rock, he shoved the Spencer out and toward the men, touching off a shot.

The bullet kicked dirt before the leading horse.

"That's far enough," he called.

"This any way to greet a friend?" asked a man with black beard and red-rimmed eyes. His grin showed broken teeth. Carty knew that face.

"Call off your dogs, Jack."

"Well, now. Reckon that depends on my dogs. What do you say, boys?"

"Hell! We can take him, seven to one."

"Four of you will die. Nogales first."

The bearded man scowled. He could see the barrel of the Spencer; he knew the man behind it could hardly miss at this distance, and his stomach contracted.

"Just rode in to share your grub."

"Don't push it. Get down from there and unbuckle your belt, nice and easy."

Nogales Jack sneered. "The hell I will."

"Don't make me pull the trigger, Jack. I'm not in a killing mood."

A man called, looking around him, "Where's the rest of them?"

"It's just me, me and the girl."

"Expect us to believe that? One man bringing her to Chessboard?"

"I'll get her there."

Nogales Jack said, "Let's talk this over."

Off to one side the grulla horse lifted its head and stared behind Carty, its ears pricked forward. Carty slid back down the rock and turned.

Two men were on the other side of the stream, bringing six-guns out of their holsters. Carty swung the rifle and fired. Then he fired again. Without looking at them, he lifted up and saw the seven riding hard for him.

His first shot knocked Nogales Jack out of the saddle; his second brought down a horse that threw its rider in a tumbling fall. The others scattered, riding hard.

A bullet snipped stone beside his ear.

He turned, seeing one of the men he had shot at leaning against a tree trunk, six-gun up and aiming. Carty flung himself sideways and clawed for his own Colt. At this distance, he told himself, he could scarcely miss. He fired, and saw the man jerk against the tree and slide down its bole. The other man lay stretched out on the ground, not moving.

There was silence.

Carty threw a glance at Kate Chance. She was backed against a cottonwood, her face white and strained. "Get down on the ground and stay there," he whispered. If those other six were going to make a fight of it, he wanted her out of sight.

Then he slid away and was gone along the stream, using the brush for shelter. He wished he had on his moccasins, but he put his feet accurately on the bottom stones, running in a crouch, his eyes sliding past the few trees and out across the flat.

The only things in sight were the dead bodies of a

horse and Nogales Jack. The others had scattered; the man who had been put afoot probably swung up onto Jack's horse and made off with the rest. Still, they might be out there, just waiting.

He scouted for almost an hour without sighting them. Might be they had turned back to meet with any others who were coming. Had Rawhide Bledsoe been among the seven? He could not be sure.

When Carty returned to where he had left Kate, he went up on the far bank to study the two dead men. He did not know either of them, had never seen them before. By rights he ought to bury them, but his loyalties were to the living. Let their friends do the spadework.

"Let's ride," he told the girl when she got to her feet.

"Is it safe?"

"Just as safe as staying here. I think they've scattered. With Nogales Jack down, they'll have to get their orders from Bledsoe. Their money, too."

They did not eat. They mounted up and rode out, and now they went at a gallop, with Carty standing in the stirrups and putting all his attention on the land around them. If they should come at him here, he would see them from far off, he would be able to reach some sort of shelter before they came within shooting range. He could ask for little more than that.

He saw no sign of them all that long afternoon.

Had they drawn back, to regroup, to plan some new method of attack? He felt certain they had. Nogales Jack was dead, so maybe there was no reason for them to keep on their trail—except for Rawhide Bledsoe, that is. He would want Kate Chance. Dead, maybe.

Carty found a little stream that went a long way and rode through it with the pack horses and Kate trailing after him. Sooner or later they would pick up his trail again, but they would be delayed, moving up and down the stream to find out where he came out.

Of course, they could get ahead of him, find a place near Chessboard, and hope he would come riding up. If Carty were after someone, that's what he would do. No sense trailing a man when you know where he's got to go, sooner or later.

He saw a stretch of rock up ahead that formed the lip of an arroyo. He had no wish to ride into that arroyo; he wanted to be able to see around him, but the rock might hide their trail a mite, and he could always go through that arroyo and come up the other side.

They came out of the stream, went across the arroyo, and now he could see a corner of the desert stretching out away from him. It wasn't much as desertland went, but the sand would hide their travel, and their canteens were full. Cut across these sands, head south by west, and after a time they ought to sight Chessboard.

It was hot. The heat didn't bother Carty at all, but Kate began to suffer. Sweat stained her outfit, and her brown hair clung to her temples where it had come loose under her hat. She drooped more and more in the saddle.

Carty would not ease up. He had to be off this sand by nightfall; they had to keep going. From time to time he eyed her, seeing her rounded shoulders, the strain in her face. She was unused to this heat, the sun glare, the dryness of the air that sucked at all the juices in a human. A Kiowa girl would still be pert and lively, but a Kiowa girl would have lived with hardship all her life.

They plodded on.

The only good thing he could say about this corner of the world was that nobody could come on them unexpectedly; he could see a far piece here, through squinted eyes. It hurt the hand to touch the iron pommel or even to hold a gun; the metal picked up that heat and held it as though you'd stuck it in a flame.

They passed clumps of barrel cactus, tall saguaro, and the scarlet flowers of red devil cactus. Kate roused from her torpor to stare at the blossoms, to remark at the weird formations of the Joshua trees.

He pointed out the reddish-brown trunks of the staghorn cholla and the flaming red clusters at the end of tall ocotillo branches, hoping to take her mind off her sufferings. She gave him a wan smile, as though she understood.

"Seems like a man could starve to death here if the thirst didn't get him first," he offered.

"You mean he wouldn't? There's nothing to eat, nothing at all. And there's no water."

He reached out for a green-and-yellow fruit growing on a saguaro and tore it loose. "Man can eat this, he gets hungry. The Papagos do. And you cut into a barrel cactus there and you'll get pulp loaded with water. A man can survive here, he knows what to do."

He talked for a long time, longer than he could remember, until they were off the desert and moving up a timbered slope. Kate straightened as she felt the coolness of the shade, lifting a hand to push at her hair, turning to give him a wan smile.

"I thank you," she said softly.

"Just talked."

"But it was interesting—fascinating, really. You say you never had any formal education, but I imagine there are men in eastern colleges who would give their eyeteeth to know what you do about Nature."

Amos Carty grinned. "Never thought about it that way. A man does what he can, what he must to stay alive in country like this."

"I know now why my brother chose you. Those other men wouldn't have all that knowledge."

"Some of them do. Most of them are town men. They travel the towns, gambling, maybe stealing some cattle when they can, or horses."

She frowned. "Are they all—thieves? Those men who consort with my brother?"

"Mostly. They're a hard lot."

"Is he—is he an outlaw?"

"Can't say."

"Or won't?" She smiled.

Carty shrugged. He had no right to run down a man to his sister, even when that man was Morgan Chance. He did not trust the man, himself. He was vaguely surprised that he thought enough of this girl to bother his head about her. The more he thought about it, the more surprise he felt. Wasn't like Morg Chance to do anything that didn't put good cash in his jeans. To his knowledge, the man had never done anything for anybody without seeing a way to profit by it.

But how could helping Kate help him?

It was a puzzle he couldn't solve.

One thing he did know, however: If Rawhide Bledsoe was anywhere around, he would make another try for him and the girl. Stood to reason. He tried to recall what he knew about the man.

He had heard of him in the saloons and along the cow trails, as men heard of other men, over bars and lonely campfires. Time was, Bledsoe had been known as Jim. But that was before he had gone up into mining country around Last Chance Gulch. He had sought to rob miners of their gold; his favorite stunt—from which he got his name—was to wrap a man up in a green hide and watch it constrict in the direct rays of the sun.

Sometimes the men talked about where their gold was hidden before the hide got too tight. Sometimes Bledsoe cut one free, then shot him; at other times, depending on his mood, he left the man in the hide until it killed him.

A mean man, Rawhide Bledsoe.

He would not be as easy as was Nogales Jack. There was animal cunning in him; he would pick and choose the place when he decided to attack. If the conditions were not right, he would back off and try again.

He was out there somewhere, waiting.

Rawhide Bledsoe pulled in his lathered horse. He had come far today, he and the men who rode with him. His eyes ranged the grasslands, seeing nothing but empty sky and equally empty land. Somewhere here, Kate Chance was riding with that unknown man.

His men drew in and surrounded him, waiting.

They were good men, from his viewpoint—hard as hickory knots, cruel, and vicious. They were not to be trusted, but neither was he. Right now he wanted desperately to lay hands on that girl, or failing that, to put a bullet into her. But he had to find her to do that.

Movement from the north caught his eye. Two horses were coming, carrying double—Little Lou Brent and Charley Woods, with Joe Haines and Waco Jimmy Blackwood behind them.

When they pulled up, it was Haines who snarled, "We found the girl, only that man with her took her away from us."

Bledsoe sat up straighter in the saddle. "You had her? And you let her go?"

Waco Jimmy Blackwood said coldly, "We didn't exactly let her go; there was a rifle on us, and we couldn't move. They took away our mounts."

Bledsoe eyed the man. "And you call yourself a gun-man?"

Haines muttered, "He was up in the rocks with a Spencer. He looked as if he wanted us to go for him."

"And you didn't?"

"No more would you, Rawhide."

"Two against one."

"It was more than two against one when Nogales Jack had them cornered. He got Nogales, he got French Jim and Larry, I hear tell."

"Who in hell *is* he?"

Lou Brent smiled coldly, pausing to draw out his Bull Durham pouch and pour tobacco into a paper. He took his time rolling the smoke, then touching it to his tongue. He was a small man, but lean and hard, and he had the reputation of being as fast a gunhand as Wes Hardin, with whom he had run for a time.

"Trouble, that's who he is," he said finally.

The others looked at him. He drew on his cigarette and let out the smoke gently. "He can go up the mountain and come down the other side, that one. He don't want to be found, you won't find him."

Rawhide Bledsoe smiled faintly. "He's put the wind up you, that's for sure."

"When he has a gun pointed at me, he surely does."

Charley Woods was staring at the smaller man. "You knew him? I saw him at that sink, but I'd never set eyes on him before."

"You let him alone, Charley. That goes for the rest of you. You ever cut his trail, you walk soft."

Bledsoe leaned an elbow on his pommel end put his eyes on the small man. Bledsoe was big, and ran to mus-cle. In his greasy shirt and battered hat he looked as craggy as a wounded puma.

"I got ten men with me. You tellin' me I should forget about goin' after that girl?"

"You'd be smart."

Rawhide Bledsoe laughed. It was a short bark of sound, with no mirth in it. "There's nobody on Earth I wouldn't tackle with you boys."

Brent shrugged. "Sure, maybe you'd get him, but you'd lose six, seven men doin' it unless you were lucky enough to dry-gulch him. If he didn't have that woman with him, you wouldn't even see that man."

Charley Woods shouted, "You've had your fun. Now who in hell is he?"

"The Indian."

Billy Joe Parsons choked. "You mean *Carty?* Amos Carty?"

"He's the one. I wonder how Morg Chance got hold of him?"

"Amos Carty," breathed the rider to the left of Bledsoe. "I seen him draw once, in a Kansas cowtown. Or maybe I should have said I seen him shoot a man." He chuckled. "I never did see his draw."

Rawhide Bledsoe scowled. He had heard tales of this man who had lived among the Kiowas. He was like a shadow flitting from here to there. He was a loner, staying much to himself in the high hills and along the back trails. Every once in a while he came into some ranch to work a spell and put money in his jeans; then he was off again, no man knew where.

"He's still only one man," he argued.

"Sure," agreed Lou Brent, dropping his half-smoked cigarette. "A bullet can kill him just as dead as anybody else. Trouble is, with Carty you got to find him to shoot him, and that ain't always easy."

"He's coming to Chessboard," muttered Bledsoe.

"And he's coming primed for gunplay."

The big man lost his temper. "We're ready for gunplay ourselves! I say we find and kill him and the girl too." His face was flushed; his eyes went around the men with him, slowly and cruelly.

Lou Brent shrugged. "You're the boss, you're the one paying the wages. But you better have a plan. You got to find Carty before you can do all you say."

Bledsoe cast a hard glance at the smaller man. If he hadn't known better, he would have thought there was a streak of yellow up and down Brent's spine. But Brent was tough, he could kill as easily as himself, he had no more conscience than a striking rattler.

Bledsoe drew a deep breath. He had no wish to anger Little Lou, he didn't want to start his men fighting among themselves. Best to calm down, to look at this from all the angles.

"We spread out first of all," he said, "and we ride for Chessboard. First one to see them two shoots off his gun. Then the others will come riding. If we don't find him at Chessboard, we turn back and ride this way, still spread out. Sooner or later one of us will find them."

Waco Jimmy said, "Me and Haines need mounts."

"We'll hit for some ranch and steal them. Meanwhile, you can double up."

Little Lou Brent was uneasy about all this. If he sighted Amos Carty he would fire off no warning shot: He would aim his gun at the Indian and shoot to kill. He hoped he would be close enough to make his shot count. He did not want to miss that first time. He might not get another chance to pull the trigger.

For two days, Amos Carty made camp at a *tinaja* where there was water and a high rock from which to scan the surrounding countryside. The horses needed rest, and so did the girl. Might be a good idea to let Bledsoe and his men run around looking for them, tire themselves out. There was no rush to get to Chessboard. The marriage could wait. Better a live bride than a dead girl.

He made smokeless fires, small ones to cook their food, and when the bacon was fried and the biscuits baked and the coffee boiled, he put out the flames by stepping on the glowing sticks rather than by pouring water on them to make steam. A man might see steam even from far off in this clear air.

On the morning of the third day they were saddled and ready to ride before dawn. He checked his loads in the Spencer repeater that held seven rounds loaded through the trap in the butt plate. His Colt held five more, and he had the extra shellbelts and guns he had taken off those two men at that ridge. He had enough bullets, but he hoped he would not have to use them.

He picked his route carefully, traveling where he could find trees, always skirting the open spaces. There were times when they had to cross open grass, but they did that at the gallop, letting the horses walk only where there was shelter.

There were times, of course, when no shelter was around, and that meant a long run where anybody with eyes could see them. Well, he had to chance that. Had he been alone he would have ridden north to come in on Chessboard from the west. He maybe ought to do that, even if it meant tiring out the girl even more.

Whatever plans he made in his mind he had to discard two hours later. A man came riding out of a draw and lifted out his rifle. He was two hundred yards away, close enough for good shooting.

"Hit the ground," Carty yelled to Kate, and then he

was yanking the Spencer and dropping over the side of his horse in the manner of the Kiowas and Comanches.

The shot that should have hit him missed by feet.

Then he was out of the saddle and lying flat, presenting as small a target as possible to the man on horseback. The grass was tall and almost hid him completely. He put the Spencer to his shoulder and squeezed off his shot, with that man framed plain to see against his sight.

The man went back off his horse and lay still.

The grulla was standing, waiting. Carty ran to it, sliding a foot into the stirrup, calling for Kate to mount up.

"They'll be around, somewhere. They'll have heard these shots."

They rode swiftly, and Carty was grateful for his decision to rest his mounts. They took off at full gallop, and now he rode with the rifle in his hands, his gaze on the barren ground around them.

There were no more shots, but over to the west he could make out two or three rising dust clouds where men were coming toward him. He understood what their plan had been, now. Scatter and find their quarry, and gunshots would be a signal.

If they waited until they were all bunched together, he and the girl would outrun them. If they came on one by one, well—they'd better shoot better than the last man.

One dust cloud was coming closer. That one rode a good horse. But the grulla and the bay mare were doing all right, he didn't want to exhaust them—they might have a grueling run before them.

"You keep on going, fast as you can," he said to Kate.

"What are you going to do?"

"Cut down the odds a little."

"No! I'd rather you stayed with me."

He smiled faintly. "You'll be all right. They're all over the place, trying to locate us. You just ride ahead."

He kept one of the spare mounts and then dismounted, moving to a rock, where he lay down and put the Spencer across it. The dust cloud was bigger; that man out there sure was in a hurry to die.

He put his cheek to the rifle and sighted.

Too far. He must wait. Well, old Buffalo Horn had taught him patience. "White men always in a hurry. Got no time to waste just sitting," he would say in his cracked voice. "Man in a hurry always makes a mistake."

This man was making a mistake. He was coming at the gallop without a thought in his head as to what might be waiting for him. Carty leaned cheek to rifle and put his finger over the trigger. Just a little more, just a little.

He squeezed off his shot.

The man went backwards, but his foot must have been caught in the stirrup, because Carty could see something bouncing and jouncing along behind the horse.

He put his eyes around the country, then. There were dust puffs to indicate where men were riding, but they were far away. He rose, and still holding the rifle, he mounted the piebald and caught up the grulla's reins.

He went off at the gallop to catch up to Kate as soon as possible. From time to time he stood in the stirrups and put his eyes around the landscape, seeing the saguaro and the Joshua trees and the ocotillo, but little else. He was lifting dust behind him, but it couldn't be helped.

He came up to Kate and made her dismount off the mare and get up on the gray. They took off again at full gallop and only slowed to walk the horses, then set off again.

Two hours later they swung back onto the grulla and the bay mare.

Carty walked off a little way at that time and ran his stare over the land. Seemed to be a dust cloud way off there to the south, but he couldn't be sure. If Bledsoe and his boys were fools enough to ride right up to Chessboard after them, why, let them. His job was to get Kate Chance safe to the man who was going to marry her. No more, no less.

When he had done that, he would ride away and be his own man again.

He discovered, as he thought about it, that his freedom did not mean so much to him as it always had. His eyes shifted toward the girl; he studied her long brown hair that had come down a little during the hard riding and that she was trying to shove up under her hat. Women always had been a mystery to him. The Kiowa women were hard workers, as were all Indian women, but these white women seemed pampered. He had seen the strain and the exhaustion in her face, in the wilting of her body. She wasn't up to hard riding, to going without food, to sleeping on the ground.

Kate Chance had taken it because there was nothing else for her to do. But he'd bet she dreamed about soft beds and tablecloths, white clean dishes on them. Anything like that would scare him.

Still, it might be time to make a change. Always in the back of his mind there had been the idea that someday he would have his own ranch. Maybe a horse ranch, with just a few cattle to provide him with beefsteaks and spending money.

He shrugged as he moved to set foot in the grulla's stirrup. No sense in thinking about all that, not with men riding after him to put lead in his body. And a girl to bring to the man who was waiting to marry her.

As they rode, he put his thoughts on Morgan Chance. He wished he knew why Morg had been so eager to have his sister stop off at Stovepipe. Morg Chance had something in his mind, all right, something to do with Kate. But what it was, he couldn't quite make out.

They rode all that afternoon, without stopping for food. There was no sign of anyone riding after them, no dust puffs marked the ground. Apparently they had come through those men Bledsoe had stretched out to find them.

At dusk they came in sight of Chessboard ranch.

CHAPTER 6

Carty sat his saddle and let the grulla blow. His eyes ranged the hill where they stood, seeing the long slope covered with rocks, the beginning of the grasslands that stretched almost as far as he could look. In the distance, he made out a group of low buildings. He turned then and studied their back trail.

Beside him, Kate Chance was restless.

"What are we waiting for?" she wondered.

He smiled thinly. "Like to know who's behind me. And who's ahead, for that matter."

"The ranch is down there. I can see it."

"Looks real peaceful, don't it?"

She studied him, vaguely angry. He was paying her no mind; he was concerned only with running those wary eyes of his around the land as if—yes! As if he were some sort of wild animal coming into new territory. She watched him scan the grasslands, the rocks, turn again to stare out over the country through which they had come, with the Chuska range behind them.

Finally he nodded and toed the grulla to a walk. She followed him, leading her spare horse. Like that they went down the slope, walking their mounts, and a tiny wind rose up to move about them. Out of the corners of her eyes, she watched Carty sniffing at it.

"Does it tell you anything?" she asked tartly.

"Yes, ma'am, it does. It tells me I'm going to be riding by myself this time tomorrow."

She opened her lips to make a remark, then caught the amusement in his eyes. She let the horses walk on a few feet before she spoke. "Are you so anxious to be rid of me?"

"I surely am, ma'am. Taking you·here has been like carrying a stick of lighted dynamite in my saddleroll."

Kate Chance straightened. "If I've been such a bother—"

"Not you. The sort of men you attract."

They rode on quietly, after that, with Kate Chance stirring restlessly in the kak, scowling at Carty behind his back. He was the most annoying man. It would really pleasure her to be rid of him.

Yet that was unfair. She realized that if it hadn't been for this man, those enemies of her brother would have taken her prisoner, might even have killed her, to strike back at Morg. Well, she was safe enough now.

They cantered across the grasslands, and by the time darkness covered the high grasses, they were within hailing distance of the ranch house. Kate felt his hand touch her arm.

"We'll wait up," he said quietly.

She reined in her bay mare and stared at him. "Whatever for? We're here, aren't we? And we're safe."

"Not yet."

His rifle was in his hands as he stepped out of the saddle to walk around and listen. Eventually he came back to where she sat the bay.

"We can go in now." He turned, and cupping a hand to his lips, called, "Halloo the house."

A door opened. Light came onto a little porch. A big man stood in the doorway.

"Kate!" he shouted, and came running.

She slid from the saddle and ran to meet him. She forgot about Carty for the moment, as she was hugged and kissed.

Peter Macklin was a big man, wide of shoulder and with lean hips. He was an Easterner who had come to love these western plains and mountains, a man who had broken his ties with New York and Philadelphia and chosen to put his money into land and cattle. His face was browned from long exposure to the Arizona sunlight, and though he still wore eastern clothes—gray-and-black-striped trousers and a matching vest over a shirt with a wing collar and a tie—he looked as fit as any of his cowhands.

He lifted his head suddenly, as though aware of Carty for the first time. There was no embarrassment in him, only good humor. He released Kate and held out his right hand.

"I'm grateful to you for bringing her to me." Curiously puzzled, his eyes went past Carty, as though seeking others who might be with them. "You came like this from the railroad?"

Carty shook his head. "We came from Stovepipe."

Macklin wrinkled his brows. "Stovepipe?"

"In the Horseheads."

"I don't understand. That's a far distance."

Carty shrugged. His eyes went about the grasslands; he knew that men such as those who had hunted this girl might be out there with perhaps a rifle lifted and ready to fire. An itching sensation formed between his shoulder blades.

"Had to be done that way. Morgan Chance has enemies who want to hit at him."

Kate shivered, then whispered, "Peter, can't we go inside?"

Macklin turned his attention from Carty to the girl. "Of course, dear. Come along. And you, too, sir."

Carty went after them, but his attention was not on

them but on the land around the ranch. He could see little; it was dark, and the slice of moon in the sky shed little light. He walked after them as silently as the wind
that touched the grasses. There was unease still inside
him, and the ranch house did little to change that feeling.

Carty mistrusted houses. They walled him in, they kept
him from seeing what lay around him in the nighttime,
they hid scents and sounds.

He said now, as he followed the others, "I'll tend to the
horses. You go on ahead."

He waited for no reply. With the reins in his hand he
took the horses around the side of the ranch and toward
the stables. There was a bunkhouse, he saw, with the yellow radiance of oil lamps coming through the windows
and the smell of cooked steaks and frying onions seeping
into the night air. He had eaten many times in bunkhouses such as this, on those occasions when he had
worked as a ranch hand to put food in his belly.

He moved with the horses past the bunkhouse and toward the huge stables off to one side. He unsaddled the
horses and lifted off the pack saddles, dropping them
close beside the building. In the barn he found an old
blanket and used it to rub down the horses.

He found containers of oats, and filled pails with water.

He waited until the horses were eating before he lifted
up his rifle and his warbag and walked toward the
bunkhouse. Before he entered it, he stood a while, listening. Then he stepped in through the doorway and faced a
long table at which six men were eating.

They paused, staring at him.

"I'm Carty. I just brought in Kate Chance to your
boss." He dropped the warbag and leaned the rifle against
the wall. He smiled faintly. "That beef and onions smells
real good."

"Didn't hear you," a tall man said, rising to his feet. "I'm Jake Albert, the foreman. This here's Joey, our wrangler, that there is Buster Jones. . . ."

The men nodded, one after another as their names were mentioned. Their eyes were wary, Carty saw, as they studied his worn buckskin jacket, the brightness of his gunbelt.

"Where's the rest of them?" a man asked.

"Just me."

Carty took off his hat, dropped it on his warbag, and moved to sit on the bench. In the kitchen he could hear the Chinese cook singing off-key, and caught the smell of meat being cooked. He sat down and leaned his forearms on the wooden tabletop.

The man called Jones looked puzzled. "Just you? To bring in the girl?"

"I was enough."

Jones pressed it. "It's a far piece from any railroad."

"Came from Stovepipe."

Surprise jerked our the words, "Just you and the girl? All that far?"

"Some men wanted to kill her to get back at her brother."

The foreman considered that. He said slowly, "He should have sent more men if he was afraid something like that would happen. He just sent you?"

"I got her here."

The Chinese cook came out with a plate heaped high with steak, onions, and fried potatoes. He put them down before Carty and trotted back into the kitchen. Carty grasped the knife and fork and began to eat.

The others sat and watched. One of them, a man with a flat face and cold, gray eyes, was smiling faintly, looking around at his companions, then at Carty. He reached for a tobacco pouch in his shirt pocket, rolled a cigarette with the ease of long practice, and then lighted it. He blew smoke for a moment.

Then he asked, "Much trouble?"

Carty chewed for a time, then said, "Killed a few men who tried to stop us."

The flat-faced man pushed it. "How many?"

"Five. One of them was Nogales Jack."

Poke Drummond blinked. He thought about what this man had said, and began to feel vaguely uncomfortable. As he watched Carty eat, his eyes narrowed slightly. All about him, the other men were looking from him to Amos Carty.

One of those men grew impatient. "I've heard of Nogales Jack. He runs with a tough crowd."

Carty finished the food and reached for the big granite coffee pot. He filled his cup, took a long drink of the hot coffee, then refilled his cup to the brim.

Then he said, "They tried to stop me."

"And there was just you?"

"Didn't need anybody else."

Drummond chuckled. "Boys, this here is Amos Carty."

"The Indian?" a man asked softly.

The youngest of the crew, a youth named Billy Andrews, hunched forward. His eyes were bright, his body quivered. Drummond slid his eyes at him and grinned.

"You really as fast as they say?" Billy asked.

Drummond said, "Billy here fancies himself with a six-gun."

"He'll get a chance to use it. Rawhide Bledsoe is coming here with more men. They want Kate Chance." Carty smiled thinly. "Up to you boys now to protect her. I've done my job."

He came to his feet easily, moved to lift his rifle and

warbag, put on the flat-brimmed Plains hat. "I'll sleep outside, or maybe in the barn."

Jake Albert protested, "No need for that. We got extra bunks."

"Man in a bunk makes a good target for a bullet."

Billy Andrew asked, "You think this Bledsoe will come here to the ranch? You think he's crazy? We got six men here."

"Bledsoe has eight. Maybe ten."

Carty was moving toward the door when he froze, turning slightly, lifting the Spencer so that its barrel covered the doorway. A moment later, Peter Macklin stepped into view. He looked at Carty, at his uptilted rifle, and his face broke into a smile.

"Kate's been telling me about you, how you got her here. You've had a bad time of it. I'd like to talk to you."

Carty nodded, lowering the Spencer.

He followed Macklin out of the bunkhouse, walking almost in his shadow, but his eyes were on both sides of the man. The night was dark, still; somewhere far off, a coyote wailed. Overhead, the stars were very bright.

Kate was sitting in an easychair as they entered. She had changed her clothes. She wore a poplin dress with a tight-fitting bodice and a round neckline, and a skirt that reached to her cloth-topped shoes. She looked a lot more relaxed, much more at home than she had out there where they had ridden.

Carty nodded at her and set down his warbag and rifle.

He said, "Just because I got you here doesn't mean you're safe."

Macklin was startled. "I have men on the ranch, Carty. Nobody would be fool enough to try to take her out of here."

"That Bledsoe's a mean man."

Peter Macklin waved a hand. "She's safe enough, I'm sure of it. But I didn't bring you here to speak about Kate's safety. I want to recompense you for what you did."

Carty shook his head. "Isn't needful. I was paying back a debt."

Macklin waved him to a chair. Carty chose a straight-back, while he himself sank into a heavily upholstered easychair. Macklin studied him a moment, frowning slightly.

"You've done me a favor, a great favor. Kate's told me about her brother, how she thinks he operates on the fringes of the law. Well, that doesn't bother me; he won't give me any trouble. The main thing is, you got her here for me to marry."

Carty waited. There was an impatience in him to be outside, where he could scan the skyline and listen for any sounds that might tell him that Bledsoe and his men would be moving in closer to this ranch. He felt penned in by the walls, the windows that were heavily draped and hung with lace curtains. A man couldn't see out of windows such as these.

"Kate and I would like you to stay for the wedding." He smiled at Carty's abrupt headshake. "However, since I gather you're a man who likes to be off by himself, I will extend the invitation even though I know you won't accept it.

"But that doesn't mean I can't show my gratitude for what you've done. Kate tells me no other man could have managed it."

"Wouldn't have been easy."

"Indeed not." Macklin looked uncomfortable. "I don't want to offend you, but I would like to offer you money—a hundred dollars, to be precise."

Carty smiled faintly. To him, a hundred dollars all in one piece was like a fortune. "I won't be offended."

Macklin rose and said, "I'll get it."

Carty was surprised. "You keep that much money here on the ranch?"

"I have a safe, a good one. A Chubb."

Kate Chance smiled. "Nobody can open it without a combination, and only Peter knows it."

Macklin left the room, and Carty glanced at Kate. She seemed like a different girl in those clothes and in this room, with its tilt-top tables—the first Carty had ever seen —and thickly tufted sofas and chairs. She was a part of the world this room represented, with its statuary on the mantelpiece, the gilt-framed pictures against the walls. She fitted in here just as his Colt fitted its holster.

Kate said, "I want to thank you, too, you know. I do appreciate what you've done." Dimples appeared in her cheeks as she added, "Despite the way I'm afraid I acted on the way here, I really do appreciate it."

"You take care," he said on impulse. "You're not out of it yet."

She looked shocked. She sat up straighter and stared at him. "Not out of it? What do you mean?"

"They'll come here. They haven't given up yet."

Kate stared at him. The color receded from her cheeks. "Are—are you trying to tell me that those men who chased us will come here to the ranch, to try to kill me?"

"I mean just that."

"You must be mistaken. Very much mistaken. Why would they do that?"

"To get at your brother."

She looked so helpless, suddenly, that Carty felt pity for her. He leaned forward. "You're smart, you and your husband-to-be will get out of here. Just as fast as you can. Get married and go live somewhere else."

"This is our home!"

"Surely is. That Bledsoe, he'll know just where to find you."

Peter Macklin came in carrying a bag. He put the bag down on a bentwood table. He counted out five twenty-dollar gold pieces, then handed them over to Carty.

"It should be more, but because no price is too high to pay for Kate's safety. But I'm a little short of hard cash at the moment. I'll get more, next time I visit a town with a bank." He smiled grimly. "There aren't very many around —banks, I mean."

"Don't want more. Don't even want this, though I'm not saying I can't use it."

Carty rose to his feet, took the gold pieces, and put them in a pocket of his buckskin jacket. He lifted his rifle and nodded at Kate, then at Macklin.

"I'll sleep out tonight. Don't care much for walls around me."

Macklin protested, but Carty shook his head. "Wouldn't sleep right in a bed, not when I know a man like Bledsoe is out there somewhere. I'll hear him better in the open."

He paused, then added, "Be better if you didn't sleep too soundly, either. That Bledsoe is a mean man."

Somewhat stiffly, Macklin said, "I'm perfectly safe here, you know. I have good men working for me."

"I'll be watching, most likely. Still, you be careful."

He went out into the night, stepping swiftly aside from the doorway, through which light was coming. It took a moment to adjust his eyes to the night darkness, but his ears needed no such change, and he heard nothing but the sounds from the bunkhouse. He toted his warbag, and his rifle was ready in his hand as he began to walk.

He was of half a mind to saddle up the grulla and ride off to the north, into Black Mesa country, without waiting

for tomorrow. Be smart to do that, get shet of these people and their troubles. His hand touched the pocket sag-
ging in the buckskin jacket with the five gold pieces.

He had taken this money, which might have been a
mistake.

He owed nothing to Morgan Chance now, nor to his
sister. By getting Kate here, he had paid that debt that
Ken Stevens had laid on him. If it hadn't been for that
gold, now . . .

He walked a mile out through the high grass before
stopping and taking his blanket from his warbag. He
wrapped the blanket around him as Buffalo Horn was
wont to do with his own blanket when he wanted
warmth, and then he lay down on the ground. His hand
reached out and brought the Spencer close in under his
hand.

He closed his eyes. He slept.

From time to time during the night Carty opened his
eyes and looked around him, listening. All he heard was
the sighing of the wind and once, very faintly, the cry of
an angry bobcat, up there in the hills. The stars looked
down; it was very peaceful. He slept, but he slept lightly,
always ready to come awake with his gun in his hand.

With the first red streaks of dawn in the eastern sky he
was up, thrusting the blanket back into the warbag, slipping feet into his boots. He rose and looked around him,
picked up the rifle first and then the warbag, and began
his walk.

A man came out of the bunkhouse, yawning and
stretching. He saw Carty and grinned. "Thought you
slept in the big house. You didn't."

"Never cared much for a bed."

"We eat in a little. Chin Lee has some eggs."

Carty paused, faintly smiling. "Eggs?"

"Boss keeps chickens in a coop, out behind a barn."

"No trouble from coyotes?"

"Brick floor, brick walls. A door two inches thick, with a lock."

Carty nodded. "Take a tough coyote to get in there."

Poke Drummond came out then, and said, "Figured you'd slept in the house."

"Slept on the grass. Safer."

Drummond opened his eyes slightly. "Safer?"

"Rawhide Bledsoe may be headed this way, with eight or ten men. Wouldn't want to wake up and find him in my room with a gun."

"You think he'll come here?"

"Wouldn't put it past him."

Carty used the pitcher of water and the bar of home-made soap. He dried his face and hands, even as his eyes scanned the vast grasslands. When he was done, he saw that Poke Drummond was close beside him, leaning against the wall of the bunkhouse.

Drummond asked, "You riding on?"

"After breakfast."

"You think Bledsoe will come here?"

"He wants to pay Morg Chance back for something, way I figure it."

Drummond thought about that, head tilted, eyes narrowed. "Won't do any good unless Chance knows about it."

Carty nodded. "Way I figure it, too."

The other man stirred. "Think I'll go see the boss and talk to him."

Carty ate the eggs and bacon, enjoying each mouthful and savoring it, but with half his mind ahead of him on the trail he would take to ride out of this basin. He would head north to the Little Colorado, hitting its waters just about where the Chevelon fork branched southward. He would ride the banks of the Little Colorado and go by way of Marble Canyon along the riverbanks to the San Juan.

After that, he would hit for Del Norte.

He had no goal in mind, he would just be riding, sleeping out under the stars. Already he could smell the sagebrush, feel the coolness of coming night strike through his clothes, baked under the western sun. A restlessness stirred in him; there was the need in him to keep riding, to make distance under the grulla's hooves.

What happened here on Chessboard was no concern of his. He liked Peter Macklin and even Kate Chance, but he was a man too used to riding alone to develop long friendships. He had done a job, nothing more.

Saddling the grulla, he saw Peter Macklin walking toward him. The man was open, friendly; he had a smile in his eyes now and a greeting on his lips.

"Had Cookie make up some grub for you, Carty. You'll take one of the pack horses."

Carty stilled his hands on the cinch buckles. "It's kind of you. I don't take a pack horse with me, usually."

"Can't go riding off without food. How would you manage?"

He smiled faintly. How could he tell this man, so used to living in a room with his favorite books at hand and his meal no farther away than a few steps, that he had gone without food for two days at such times when the hunting was not there, and drank sparingly from his canteen because there might not be a waterhole nearer than forty miles?

"Appreciate it," he nodded.

Macklin hesitated. "I don't suppose you'd care to stay on? Hire yourself out to me as a range rider? Not to brand cows or ride herd, but just to keep an eye on things?"

Macklin wanted a hired gun.

Well, Carty could understand that. He had hired out his gun to other ranches, at various times in his life. He had fought in a range war or two, but only because he rode for the brand. He was not about to take on the job of salaried gunman for wages.

Carty shook his head, but he smiled. "I'm a wanderer. I like the high places to sleep in, the cool wind blowing across the mountain peaks. The loneliness. But I'm obliged."

He went on tightening the cinch, knowing Macklin was watching him, frowning a little trying to think of something to say that might make him change his mind.

"A hundred a month and your keep," Macklin announced finally.

Carty sighed. A hundred a month was a lot of money, even for a fast gun. He could do the job Macklin wanted done, all right. He could rove this grassland until he came upon Bledsoe and his gunfighters, and he would eliminate them, one by one—or two by two, if that was the way the cards fell. But there was that restlessness in him, alive now and pulling at him, that told him he must be moving on.

He said slowly, "I appreciate it. Some other time, maybe. Now I have the need in me to be off by myself." He hesitated. "That money you gave me last night. It has nothing to do with that. I'll give it back if . . ."

Macklin cut in, "You will like hell. That money's yours. I wouldn't have it any other way." He waited, then asked, "What do you think I ought to do? I didn't figure when I fell in love with Kate that I'd be taking on men who hate her brother."

"Get her away from here."

Macklin shook his head. "I can't do that. I've pulled up all my roots. This is my home now, this ranch. I'll fight for it."

"Nobody's after the ranch. Just Kate."

Peter Macklin nodded gloomily. He looked down at his hands, widening his fingers, then clamping them into big fists. "Guess I can protect her. I'd be a poor husband if I couldn't."

"Can you use a gun?"

"I'm reasonably good with a rifle."

"Then keep it handy."

Carty swung up into the saddle, waved a hand, and toed the grulla into a walk. The pack horse came after him, its reins in his hands. He headed northward away from the ranch buildings, across the grass sea waving slightly in the breeze. Once he turned in the kak and stared back. Macklin was still standing there, looking after him.

Uneasiness rested in Carty. He liked Macklin, and he was a man who did not cotton to people. He felt sympathy for the man. Wasn't his fault if the woman he loved had a brother who had enemies. Been him, he'd have sent Kate back East until he could rid himself of those men who were after her—or better, go get Morgan Chance and turn him over to Rawhide Bledsoe.

He smiled faintly at that notion. It would take a bit of doing, that. Morg surrounded himself with gunmen, same as Bledsoe did.

Be fun to get them all together, then duck out of sight.

The grulla made good time across the grasslands, into the low hills that skirted the northern boundary of the ranch. Carty rode easily, without any need for hurry inside him. He eased in the kak and let his eyes roam the foothills, scan the creosote bushes off to one side, the yellow blossoms of the prickly pear.

He loved the vast loneliness of this land. The sky was an empty blueness overhead; there seemed no end to it. Wherever he put his gaze, he saw no living thing outside himself and his two horses. This was the way he wanted it, alone and without any obligations to hinder him in his goings.

After a time he built a cigarette from the Bull Durham pouch in his buckskin pocket. His fingers touched the gold coins. He made his smoke and enjoyed it, but the touch of that money was a memory that disturbed him. He had done what he had out of an old friendship for Ken Stevens. He would not be drawn any farther into the lives of these people.

He walked onto an edge of the Painted Desert and moved slowly, the heat baking him and his horses. The colors of the sands were never-ending delights to his eyes, and he seeped himself in that hot beauty for a long time. The air was pink at times, it seemed, then purple. Colors seemed to wash across these sands in waves: There were amethyst and gold, pale lilac and russet. It was like moving in a fairyland.

He stopped the grulla to enjoy the mesas that were bathed in tinted hues. A man had told him once that some of those colors came from the limonite and hematite in the rocks. Whatever their cause, they were a pure pleasure to the eyes.

He came up the Little Colorado at nightfall and made his camp.

He would have preferred a higher place. He was open here, exposed to view. Yet the river was beautiful in the moonlight, and a man could sit by its bank and think his own thoughts. He made a small fire and cooked his meat, made biscuits from river water and the flour that Macklin had given him. He made a pot of coffee and finished it, lazing near the river.

Next morning he was up at dawn, making more coffee and chewing on the meat he had cooked last night and set aside. He saddled the grulla and put the pack back on the lead horse.

All that day he kept to the riverbank, riding slowly. He was in no hurry; nothing waited on him. He was like an animal in that regard, he guessed. When there was nothing to occupy him, he lazed. Once, when the heat at noon was close to intolerable, he swung down, stripped the saddles from the horses and the clothes from himself, and took them with him into the water.

The water was cold; it felt good to his parched skin. He swam about, sat naked on the sand, and just plain loafed. He was going nowhere in particular. What was the sense of rushing? He stayed all that day at the river, swimming and coming out to dry, then going in again.

That night he ate the rest of the food the Chinese cook had prepared for him. Then slept dreamlessly, soundly.

Two days later, he was in the hills bordering the San Juan.

He was swinging down from the grulla behind a stand of cottonwoods when he saw the riders. He put his fingers to his horses' nostrils to stop them from whinnying as his eyes studied the line of men riding slowly along a cutbank.

The man in the lead was Morgan Chance.

CHAPTER 7

Carty watched those men, but only out of the corners of his eyes, because a direct stare can sometimes alert a man to the fact that he is being watched. He frowned slightly, wondering where Chance was riding with this gunmen at his back.

To attend the wedding of Kate Chance and Peter Macklin?

He did not think so. Morg Chance was no sentimentalist.

Then why were they here—and coming from the north?

It was a puzzle. Also, it was no affair of his.

Still, he watched those men, seeing Hobe Talbert and Pike Shattuck. Ed Wells was there too, along with Pud Henry. Carty's eyes watched them, saw how they moved steadily southward. They had a goal in mind, all right.

Nothing to rob very close to here, though. Not much of anything, in these parts.

He waited until the dust their horses' hooves raised had settled down before he unsaddled and made his camp. He had shot a mule deer earlier; he cut it up now and put two thick slices on the fire. The rest he would cook later, at his leisure, and wrap it in a meat tarp that the Chinese cook had put on the pack saddle.

Carty settled his back against a rock and ate his food. As soon as he was finished he covered the fire with dirt. His coffee was hot; he would finish it in darkness. He had

no way of knowing how far away Morg Chance and his
men might be, and he did not want them nosing around
him because of a fire.

When it came time to sleep, he took his blanket and
walked high into the hills, leading his horses until he came
to a flat, grassy meadow. He lay down with the Spencer
in his hand and slept.

Next morning he saddled up and rode east, toward Del
Norte.

Morgan Chance sat up, reaching for his boots. He was
at peace with his world; another two days would see him
on his sister's ranch. She ought to be married by that
time, if Pete Macklin was any kind of eager bride-
groom. He would have to find out about that wedding.
No sense riding in if she wasn't a wife.

He thought about that as he moved to the fire where
Pike Shattuck was bent above the flames. Do no good to
show up if Kate wasn't safely hitched to that Easterner.
His plans depended on that.

He put his stare on the river, watching the water move
by, then lifted his eyes to regard the rough country
through which they were riding. There were cottonwoods
here beside the river, but out there, where they would be
going, was only saguaro cactus and burro bush. He was
tired of looking at cactus and burro bush. He wanted a
fine bed to sleep in, herds of cattle to call his own, a ranch
where he could set up the lifestyle he dreamed of.

There would be no more robbing and riding, fleeing
vengeful posses.

Not for Morg Chance, there wouldn't. Nobody knew
him, down there in Arizona—except Rawhide Bledsoe
and Nogales Jack, of course.

He pondered about them, wondering if the Indian had

gotten Kate safely through. If he hadn't, this ride was a fool's errand. Still, his money was on Amos Carty.

Hobe Talbert came up beside him, sniffing at the cooking meat, then running his stare at Chance.

"What you think?" he asked. "She there?"

"There or dead."

"She's sure no good to us dead."

Morg grunted. He knew that, well enough. Everything depended on how the Indian had done. If any man could do it, the Indian could. He'd said that before, and he would stick to it.

"He got through," he muttered now.

Hobe Talbert thought about that, eying the meat that was cooking. "What about this Macklin? How tough is he?"

"Not tough enough to stop a bullet."

"He has men riding for him."

Morgan Chance turned and looked at him. "You want out?"

"Hell, no. I'm just thinking."

"I'm Kate's brother, ain't I? I show up to wish them good luck in their marriage. You boys take care of her husband. When she's a widow—well, hell. I just can't ride off and leave her in her sorrow, can I?"

Hobe chuckled. "Wouldn't be fittin'."

"So I stay on. I bring you boys in to help me. Pretty soon we're running that ranch—for Kate, it'll seem like. For a time."

"What about her? Your own sister?"

"If she's smart, she'll let me ramrod her outfit. No reason why she shouldn't, me being her brother and all."

Morgan Chance reached for a piece of meat Pike extended to him. He chewed and swallowed. No more of these lonely campfires for him, no more sleeping out with the sky overhead. That was all right for Amos Carty. He was half an animal, anyhow.

For Morgan Chance there was to be a ranch, a bedroom with clean sheets, and a big living room where he could stretch out and take his ease while others worked for him, making that ranch pay off. He chewed some more. Kate might yell a little, kick up her heels. But he knew how to handle her.

If need be, he'd cuff some sense into her—not gently, either. Kate needed a firm hand, and his was the hand to do it. Might be a good idea to get her married to some man like Pike Shattuck or maybe Pud Henry. Not Hobe. He didn't trust Hobe Talbert.

Morg drank the hot coffee, moving around, watching where Pud Henry was saddling the horses. Pud was a good boy; he listened to Morgan Chance and did what he was told without asking questions. Man like that would be easy to handle.

Morg waited until they had all eaten, then swung into the kak. He led the way along the riverbank, then on up onto higher ground. They would follow the river down into Arizona Territory, be sure of having plenty of water when they wanted it.

They were in no hurry.

Kate had to be a married woman before they could move in.

The eight men rode toward the little town in the long shadows of coming night. They walked their horses out of the pines, and their eyes studied the saloon, the livery stable, and the few other buildings that made up a town. They did not know its name, nor did they care. There would be liquor in it, and their throats were dry from their long riding.

"No foofaraw, now," Bledsoe stated. "Don't pick any fights, don't cause any attention. We eat and we drink a little, and that's it."

"Be a good idea to do some talking," murmured Lou Brent.

Bledsoe eyed the man to his right. "Talk about what?"

"That there ranch. Wouldn't hurt none to know how many men we're going up against. What do you know about that place where Carty took that woman?"

"All I know is, she's there."

Lou Brent slid his stare at the big man. "You're stupid, Rawhide. That stuff you're named for has more brains than you."

Bledsoe reined in his big bay. There was a coldness in him as he looked at the smaller man, who was smiling faintly. "You trying to pick a fight?"

"Not with you, not with anybody. I'm plumb peaceful."

Bledsoe eyed him. "You don't sound it, not the way you talk."

"I like to know what I'm up against before I go for my gun."

"What's that mean?"

"Carty's got the girl to that ranch by this time. They have tongues, the both of them. Granted the Indian doesn't talk much, but there's no bridle on that girl. She saw what happened."

The big man scowled. "So?"

"So she's warned that man of hers that somebody was hunting for her. If you were that man, what'd you do?"

"Fort up. Hire some gunmen."

Brent shrugged. "There you are. You may get fun out of riding in there as if you were leading a cavalry charge, but I'm a man who likes his skin too much for anything like that."

They walked to the tierail in front of the saloon before Bledsoe spoke again. As he swung a leg over the cantle, he asked, "What would you do if you were after that Chance woman?"

"Give her a longer lead rope. Let a week pass. A couple of weeks. There ain't no rush, is there?"

"And so?"

"Soon as she feels there'll be no more trouble, she'll go riding out over that range, maybe with her husband, maybe without him."

It made sense, the big man reflected as he moved toward the saloon. There was no need for haste in him; it was Morgan Chance he wanted, not his sister. The girl was only a means to an end. Could be that Little Lou had him some good thoughts about that.

"We'll wait," Bledsoe muttered, as he pushed open the batwing doors.

The saloon was a single long room, flanked on one side by a bar, with tables here and there, and in the rear, a faro layout and an empty card box. Bledsoe gave the layout a mere flick of the eyes. He was no gambler, other than for a friendly game of stud poker. When he chose to risk something, he did it on what he considered to be pretty much of a sure thing.

He moved to the bar, where the men were already bellied up, and he watched the barkeep moving to lift bottles and glasses and set them before the drinkers. When the man finally turned to him, Bledsoe gave him a curt nod as he reached for the bottle.

"Much play here?" he asked, jerking his head at the faro table.

The bartender grinned. "Boys from a couple of ranches come in to take their chances, every so often. This Paydirt town grew up when they found some silver back in the hills. The silver petered out, but the town hung on because of the ranches."

Bledsoe drank slowly, carefully, sipping the liquor. It was cheap whiskey, raw and burning to the throat. He put down his glass.

"Got a place for my boys to stay, maybe a few days or a week?"

"Old man named Ike Johnson runs a hotel—if you can call it that." The bartender ran his eyes down the line of men. "Some of your crew might have to double up, even sleep three in a bed, but I guess Ike can manage it."

Bledsoe lifted the bottle and carried it and the glass to a table that gave him a view of the street. He sat down and sipped, and thought about Kate Chance and the man called Carty.

Bledsoe had to hand it to the Indian. He'd done what Rawhide Bledsoe would never have believed possible. The question now was: Had Amos Carty stayed on at the Macklin place? Bledsoe would scout around, send out his men to ask questions. Until then, he was satisfied to sit and wait.

Maybe Brent was in the right of it, after all.

Five days later, Amos Carty was in the San Luis Valley, moving eastward toward the Sangre de Cristo mountain range. Far north of those mountains, close by South Pass, was the little cabin he and his father had built so long ago. He would go there, look the place over, and make any repairs that had to be made, then settle in for the rest of the summer, plan to do some hunting during the fall, and put down trap lines for the winter. Might be he could make himself a little money in furs, come the cold weather.

He still fretted some about Kate Chance, but her mem-

ory was fading from his mind the farther away from
Chessboard he rode. A woman was not for him. He was a
loner, content to ride the backwater trails, the high country, always by himself. A man like him had nothing to
offer any woman.

Might be a good idea to ride into one of the little towns
that dotted the Arkansas or its tributaries like the Purga-
toire or the Aphishapa and get himself a woman. Spend a
few days or nights with her before riding on. Take the
tensions out of him.

There was a backwater town not far from here, just beyond La Veta Pass, not far from the Huerfano River.
What was it called? He had visited it some years back,
after his father had been killed by the Sioux. He had been
a youngster back then, he had been thinking of riding
back to a Kiowa encampment and spending the rest of his
life with them.

Jackpot. That was its name.

Carty smiled faintly. It had seemed like quite a place to
him, after having known only the Kiowa tipis and that
cabin he and Pa had built. Two saloons, even a building
that men called a hotel. There had been women in the saloons, women at whom he had hardly dared look.

It had been in Jackpot that he had met Ken Stevens.

Stevens had been as footloose as himself. They had
teamed up together to ride to one of the ranches down in
the Llano Estacado country. They had worked there for a
couple of years until the need to move on hit Carty. He
had rarely worked as a ranch hand after that, content
with living in the high country, fishing and hunting, putting together some furs during the winter season and
selling them for hard cash.

Be good to ride into Jackpot. It would bring back
memories.

He turned eastward at San Luis Lake and went over the Sangre de Cristos.

He came into Jackpot in late afternoon, walking his horses through the dusty street, seeing the hotel and the two saloons as smaller and meaner than he had remembered them. They were sunbaked, parched. A few horses were before the tierail, and off on a little hillside he could make out what appeared to be a graveyard. He was a little surprised at that, and reined in to study it.

"Didn't know Jackpot had that many people," he muttered.

He eased from the saddle, tie-reined his horses to the pole, and stood a moment, staring at the mountains to the west, and the vast plains all around. Sunlight glinted on the waters of the Huerfano. Then he stepped up onto the porch and moved through the batwings into the heat of the big room.

Heads turned to glance at him, but he paid them no mind after a quick glance at each face. He saw a girl sitting over at a table with two men who looked vaguely like miners, but he ignored her for the moment.

"You got any milk?" Carty asked.

The barkeep opened his lips to laugh, but he choked his mirth back after his eyes studied the brown face and long yellow hair of the man before him. Memory stirred in the bartender; something out of the far past nudged his streak of caution. Where had he seen this man before? There was something about him, something that jarred at his nerves.

"Might find some at the hotel," he said.

Carty nodded, and turned to glance at the girl. She was new to him; he'd never seen her before. She was pretty, she was young, and that yellow dress she wore clung to her body like wet silk.

Carty recalled a name he had heard, that other time when he had been here with Ken Stevens. Stevens had been sweet on that other girl, and even he himself had admired her from a distance.

"Nora not here any more?" he asked.

"You go back a ways. Nora found some cowhand who wanted to marry her, so she went off with him. She ain't been here for five, maybe six years."

Carty nodded, and pushed away from the bar.

The man behind the bar watched him go, reaching for a glass to polish with a dry cloth. Now, what did he know about that yellow-haired stranger? He had been here before; he knew about Nora. Fred Baxter settled himself to some heavy thinking, leaning against the bar.

A lean man who had stood watching Carty, moved along the bar. "Who is he, Fred?"

"Don't know, but he knew Nora."

"She's been gone a long time." The man, who wore his six-gun tied low, hunched forward. "Funny. He didn't ask for a drink."

"He wanted milk."

"*Milk?*"

The lean man turned to shout something to his friends, but the voice of the barkeep halted him. "Wait, Jim. Don't start trouble with him."

Jim Young swung back, staring. "Why not?"

"There's something about him. I'm trying to remember. It ain't nice. He keeps sticking in my craw, but I can't quite fasten onto what is is about him."

"Don't look like much."

The barkeep sighed. "Neither does a stick of dynamite before it goes off."

The lean man snorted.

Carty walked his horses to the hotel and took them

around back into a dilapidated barn. He removed their saddles, rubbed them down, found some grain and water for them, then moved toward the hotel. There was a man sleeping in a chair, he saw as he entered.

Carty went behind the counter, lifted a key from the rack, and signed his name. He carried his warbag up the stairs, opened the door, and walked into the room. His eyes ran from the bed to the washstand. Might be a good idea to shave before he went to see a woman.

He shaved, he washed as much of the grime from him as he could, and he thought about a bath. Hadn't been for his hankering to be with a woman tonight, he would have slept out there on the ground. Women were fussy creatures.

He lay down on the bed and slept for an hour, waking refreshed.

He went down the narrow staircase and into the dining room. There were half a dozen men there, bent over their plates, who glanced at him, then turned back to their food. Carty took a chair at a table near a window.

A man came shuffling across the floor to serve him steak and potatoes. Carty ate quietly, his mind on the evening ahead. He would go the saloon, buy drinks for that woman (he had to have some himself, he guessed), and he would hire her services for the night—if she was available, that is. Could be that other men would be ahead of him—after all, he was a stranger in town.

He paid for his meal and walked out into the night's darkness. He kept to the shadows, which were deeper and darker where the buildings loomed, and he used his eyes. Jackpot was smaller than he remembered. There were still the same number of buildings, but he had been younger then, he hadn't seen much of the world—not that he had seen all that much since, at that.

Carty angled his walk toward the saloon.

He went into a haze of smoke and a smell of liquor.
Riders from off the ranches to the south had come in;
their horses were lined up against the long tierail. The
bartender was kept busy, so Carty used his eyes to scout
the big room. He saw the girl in the yellow dress laughing
with some men at a table, and now he saw two more
women in low-cut dresses talking with some of the cowhands.

Carty leaned against the bar. The bartender glanced at
him, nodded, and pushed a bottle in his direction. Carty
poured sparingly. He hunched his elbows on the bar, almost as if protecting the liquor in the glass.

He did not want to drink, but he was going to have to,
if only to get the nerve to go over to one of those girls and
strike up a talk. He wasn't much of a hand with white
girls. He could talk to the Kiowas; he was a lot more at
ease with them. Too bad one of those girls wasn't an Indian.

After a moment, he stirred. There were eyes fastened
on him, he knew that sensation. He turned a little from
the bar and ran his gaze around the room.

A lean man was staring at him, eyes hard.

"You come far?" the lean man asked.

"Far enough."

"You ridin' on?"

Carty smiled thinly. The lean man was half drunk, and
he was pushing for trouble. Carty wanted no trouble, he
wanted a woman. He merely shrugged and looked down
at his glass.

The lean man waited, then he said, "You didn't answer
me."

It was then that the bartender looked up. He saw Carty
move slightly, away from the bar. And memory rushed

back to him. It had been a long time ago, six years or more, but it had been on a night like this when Rand Pearson and two of his cowhands had come into his bar, hunting trouble.

Rand had always fancied himself with a Colt. He had seen two young strangers and had decided that they were ripe for the plucking. They had been alone, they had been talking, when Rand had stepped over to their table. He himself had been busy, he hadn't heard what Rand had said, but he had been alerted when a sudden silence had fallen on the room.

Rand and his two cronies had gone for their guns.

This man with the yellow hair hadn't seemed to move, but his gun was out, firing, and Rand Pearson and his two men were falling. . . .

"Hold it, Jim," he said now.

Jim Young did not take his eyes away from Carty, but he asked, "What for?"

"I remembered, Jim. This man is Amos Carty."

The lean man blinked. "The Indian?"

"Some folks call him that."

Carty waited quietly. He had no desire to shoot down this man who was primed for trouble. All he wanted was a warm, loving woman. He saw the man called Young lick his lips and try to smile.

"Just trying to be friendly," he muttered.

"Sure," said Carty. "Have a drink."

Jim Young nodded and moved against the bar. Talk began again in the room; Carty could hear the click of poker chips. He pushed money across the bar and watched as the barkeep filled the glass in front of Young.

The bartender eyed Carty a moment.

"Took me some time to remember you, but I did."

Carty nodded. "Been a while."

"Guess you come here to visit that friend of yours—his grave, I mean."

Carty felt the tenseness come up inside him. "Friend of mine? You mean Ken Stevens?"

"That's the one."

Carty turned the whiskey glass around in his fingers. "How long ago did he die?"

"Six, eight months, about then."

"Who killed him?"

"Man by the name of Talbert. Hobe, I think it was. He had friends with him, but he done his own shooting."

"Sure about that?"

"Didn't see it, myself. This Talbert, he came in one morning, said that Stevens had called him, and that he'd shot him in self-defense. His two pals backed him up." The barkeep shrugged. "Wasn't any business of mine. And this two-bit town doesn't have any marshal."

Six months ago, Carty had been in Green River country, up in Wyoming. He had brought in a good haul of furs to Fort Laramie and sold them to a dealer for gold that he had ridden to Denver to bank. Been after that when he'd met that stranger down in San Carlos country who'd told him Ken Stevens had gone west into California.

His smile was bitter.

Morgan Chance had set him up, real neatly. He had gambled on the fact that Amos Carty would come in to him, and he had done what Morg had expected. Chance had sent Talbert and those other men to make certain that Ken Stevens would never show up. But why? Just to get Amos Carty to take Kate Chance to Arizona? Didn't seen to make much sense.

Morgan Chance didn't give a hoot in hell about his sister, unless—

He brooded, hunched over the glass of whiskey. Men came and went in the saloon, they raked him with their eyes, but he paid them no heed.

Morg Chance was riding into Arizona now.

Just to visit Kate?

That didn't make any sense, either.

Peter Macklin had him a good ranch, with plenty of graze, plenty of cattle. He was on the way to becoming a rich man in a few years. Just suppose now that Morg Chance should appear and find some way of taking over that ranch for himself.

Carty straightened.

His hand pushed the glass of whiskey from him. No time to be drinking now. He had him something important to do. His eyes touched the girl in the yellow silk dress. Carty sighed. No time to be thinking of women, either.

He walked away from the bar, moved out into the night.

In the shadows of the saloon, he studied the hillside graveyard. He would go there and look down at the grave of Ken Stevens. He wanted to make sure Stevens was dead.

But not now. Not at night.

He walked back to the hotel and went up the stairs. If he were right in his suspicions, he was going to go back into Arizona. He wanted to have a talk with Morgan Chance, with or without the gunslicks he kept always at his elbow. Might be a good idea to tell Peter Macklin about Morg Chance, too, to warn him.

Right now, he would sleep.

He ate three eggs and half a pound of bacon for breakfast, with biscuits and four cups of coffee. He paid his bill and carried his warbag out to the barn, where he saddled up the grulla and put the pack on the pinto. He swung up into the kak and walked the horses down the main street and up onto the grassy little hill that was the local grave-yard.

He grounded the reins and walked among the clumps of grass, staring at the wooden crosses. When he came to one that read "K. STEVENS," he took off his Plains hat and ran his eyes over the mound.

Stevens had been a good friend. There had been a laughing, carefree quality about him that Carty, suffering at the time from the loss of his father, had cottoned to. Ken Stevens had supplied something that he himself lacked—a boyishness, a sense of fun, and a quick ability to laugh, maybe.

They had cut their trails a long time ago, but the memories lingered in Carty, with a certain sadness. He felt a vague desire to say a prayer or something like it, something appropriate, but he knew no prayers.

"Luck," he whispered, and turned away.

He mounted up and rode away without looking back. Arizona Territory was several sunups away, and he had business with Morgan Chance in Arizona Territory.

CHAPTER 8

He rode through the long sunlight, through the wide fields of grass, heading for Wolf Creek Pass, which would take him through the San Juans and toward the Los Pinos River. There was no hurry in him. Whatever was happening down there on Chessboard ranch would take place, no matter what he did. He could stop nothing, not here on the Colorado plains.

From time to time he swung off the grulla and onto the pinto. The pinto was a smaller horse, but it could go until it dropped. Always he kept to the edge of the low hills when he could, and his eyes were always active.

He was coming out of Cheyenne and Arapaho country soon, down into where the Kiowas ran, and sometimes the Apaches. He had no fear of the Kiowas, he was one of them—or so regarded himself—but those Apaches were another story. He didn't want to be caught on any flat with the Ta'gua'kia after him.

When he came to the mountains, he breathed a little easier. He could hide himself in the mountains if need be. Take a good tracker to find him when he did, too. He moved in among the juniper and box elder and began his climb. From time to time, over the soft places, he ran out his rope and dragged it behind him to obliterate his tracks.

He made camp high in the timberline, where lodgepole pine and Douglas fir grew. He built his fire behind some rocks, and he used old, dry wood to avoid making much smoke. Even as he cooked his meat, he was moving restlessly to the edge of the ravine beside which he had his fire. Nobody could come at him from the ravine; it was too steep.

He ate and drank his coffee, then put out the fire.

In the darkness, with the stars overhead, he sat with the wind murmuring about him, and Amos Carty thought. Not much sense in Morg Chance riding down into Arizona Territory unless he meant to do something to put money in his jeans. Carty knew that much about the man. Nor was he going alone, but backed by men who wouldn't hesitate to kill if it meant profit. Even without the profits, just for the sheer hell of it.

It had to be the ranch. Made no sense, otherwise.

Chance was going to visit his sister and her new husband. Sooner or later, something was going to happen to Peter Macklin. Morg would be there to give his shoulder to Kate to cry on.

After that . . .

Carty pursed his lips, whistling soundlessly. He was beginning to understand a little of what was going on, what was about to happen. Funny he hadn't seen it before—but then, he hadn't known about Ken Stevens being gunned down.

They must have murdered him, one way or the other. Stevens was no fast gun, but he had sand, and he would stand up to a man like Hobe Talbert. But if Talbert had friends to side him, somewhere so Stevens hadn't seen them, Stevens wouldn't have had a chance.

It had been murder, he was sure of it.

Nobody had seen the killing except Talbert and his cronies. They could have told any story they wanted. There had been no law in Jackpot then. Still wasn't.

Carty came down off the San Juans and held the grulla straight for the river. There was an anger in him, slow-burning and smoldering, but still there. It wasn't only the fact that Morg Chance had played him so neatly, getting him to take his sister to Chessboard ranch, it also was the fact that he had sent men to kill Ken Stevens so Stevens couldn't possibly have paid Chance the money Chance said he owed him.

He owed Morg for that.

All that long day and for the day after, Carty rode through the San Juans, until he came down off them and headed for the Animas River. He changed mounts, shot a brace of rabbits for his supper, and cooked them in sight of the Carrizo Mountains. He would be in New Mexico Territory when he reached those high hills, and Arizona Territory was just a long jump away.

Two days later he was close to the Painted Desert.

He came toward the Macklin spread cautiously. It was never in his mind to rush into things blindly. He did not intend to ride up to that ranch house, making a target a child could hit with a gun. His way was the Kiowa way. He would circle about and investigate, then make his plans.

He saw cattle, he saw men at a distance holding those cattle, and he moved away from them, always keeping a hillock or a clump of trees between him and the riders. He wanted no man to see him unless he was ready. The ranch house was quiet; he saw no signs of life about it.

Carty turned the pinto then, and rode away with the grulla trotting after him. He found an arroyo and went along it for some distance, then came up on the far side and headed for some hills.

He was moving across the flatland when he saw the horse.

It was standing, ground-reined, tail idly swishing. Where there was a saddled horse, this far out on the range, there was also a man. Carty came out of the kak with his Spencer in his hand, and dropped flat along the ground. He waited with the Spencer ready to fire, while his eyes roved the grassland.

From time to time that bay horse lifted its head and looked at something on the ground, not far away. After a glance, it dipped its head toward the grasses.

Carty began his crawl.

He went as he had been taught by old Buffalo Horn, slowly and with a care not to make a noise. After a time, he began to get a feeling. He did not rise to his feet, but he crawled faster, and when the horse turned and looked at him, he stood up.

He walked through the grass to where a man made a motionless heap.

It was Peter Macklin—he lay face down, and there was blood on his hide vest. Carty knelt beside him after glancing around, and put the Spencer on the ground. He studied the wound.

"Backshot," he muttered, and turned the man over.

Macklin opened his eyes. He stared at Carty.

"Was it you shot me?" he asked weakly.

Carty shook his head. He wasted no time on words; he stripped away the shirt and vest, and reached for some grass, which he wadded into a ball and with it tried to stop the flow of blood.

"Been me shooting, you'd be dead," he said after a time, and rolled Peter Macklin over on his front.

The bullet had gone in through his lung, but it had missed the heart. Macklin had lost blood and was very weak. He needed a doctor, a bed, and a long period of convalescence, but maybe he would make it.

Carty did what he could with the grass. The bullet had

gone through the man, at least. He wouldn't have to probe for it with his knife. When he had thrust the grass in that wound, he sat back on his heels.

"Your ranch is too far away to take you there. Any other place you know of where I can get you into a bed?"

Macklin said something that Carty had to lean closer to hear. The man was weak; in a few seconds he would lose consciousness. After a time he made out the words Macklin was trying to say.

A line cabin—west of here, near the breaks.

"Got to get you on your horse," he said.

Macklin nodded, and with Carty lifting him, rose to his feet, where he swayed back and forth. Carty supported him and brought him to his horse, which shied at first but stood at Carty's words. Macklin put a foot into the stirrup.

"Can't—make it," he panted.

Carty got under him and boosted him. When he was in the kak, Carty took his rope and fastened his hands to the horn. Macklin drooped, his head fell to his chest, but he stayed upright.

Carty went for his own horses, then mounted up on the grulla, and taking the reins of Macklin's horse, walked them westward. He put his stare on the breaks he could see, far off across the grasslands. Those breaks marked the westernmost boundary of the ranch, he guessed. The line cabin would be somewhere near them.

He came up on it with an hour of daylight left. It was a small cabin made of logs chinked together with dried clay, with a door and one window. Riders for the ranch could stay here and not travel all the way back to the ranch bunkhouses when they were working this corner of the range. There was a chimney fashioned of stone on the north side.

Carty dismounted and opened the door. One quick

glance showed him four bunks built into the walls. There
were folded blankets on each bunk, but no pillows.

He helped Macklin out of the saddle and brought him
into the line cabin. He made him sit on an empty bunk
while he spread blankets over another. Then he lifted him
and helped him across the room.

"You get between them blankets, and you stay there.
Go to sleep. I'll cook up some grub, but you won't feel
like eating for a time."

When Macklin was on his back with the blankets
folded around him, Carty moved to the door and out of it,
stepping sideways. It was dark now, with the moon and
the stars overhead and the fragrance of sagebrush in the
air. Whoever had shot Macklin was long gone, Carty
figured, but he would take no chances.

He unsaddled the horses and picketed them on long
ropes, within reaching distance of a little stream that ran
sparkingly clear water over its bottom stones. Then he
went for his pack and rounded up some dry wood from an
overhang behind the cabin.

He made a fire in the fireplace, and on the flames he
cooked what was left of an antelope he had shot two days
before. He also found a pot and filled it with water, dropping what meat he had left into it, to make a soup. The
soup he would save for Macklin when he woke.

When he was done eating he left the cabin, taking his
own blanket and moving through the darkness until he
came to a stretch of flat ground somewhat higher than the
rest. He lay down, wrapped himself up, and fell asleep.

Dawn saw him moving toward the cabin.

There would be searchers out soon. Kate would be
missing her husband, and either she would be riding or
her men would be, hunting for him. Could be that Morgan Chance and his boys would also be doing some look-

ing. They knew where to find the body, the way he had it figured.

Macklin was awake as he walked in.

"I'm weak," he said. "Damned weak."

"You stay right there. No need for you to go anyplace. I'll heat up that soup I made last night. Maybe make some biscuits, too."

"You'll find flour in the larder. We keep a supply there for the boys who come here."

Macklin was unable to feed himself, so Carty did the job, sitting on the edge of the bunk. The food seemed to strengthen Macklin, for his voice grew stronger and his eyes seemed clearer after he had eaten. He lay and watched Carty prepare his own food.

"Thought you were riding out," Macklin said when Carty was drinking coffee.

"Rode out, all the way to Jackpot, somewhere west of the Sangre de Cristos. Learned that a friend of mine had been shot down about eight months ago.

"That bring you back?"

Carty sipped coffee. He made a cigarette, lighted it, and blew smoke.

"You know your wife's got a brother? Kate is your wife by this time, isn't she?"

Macklin smiled faintly. "She is. We got married the day you left. I had never met that brother of hers. But then, a day or two later, he came riding in big as life. He's at the ranch house now."

"And you're shot up."

Macklin stared. He tried to rise up on an elbow, but the pain lanced through him, and he sank back. He asked, "You don't mean to tell me you associate those two events?"

"You better watch out; you'll lose your ranch to that

man. He's mean and he's got no conscience. Wasn't Morg who did the shooting; he left that to some of his cronies. But he's behind it."

"I—I don't understand."

"He had you shot. That leaves Kate, who had no part of this. But she's a woman, and she's alone. When they bury you, the way they planned, Morg will stay on. He'll bring in his men to run that ranch."

Macklin stared up at the ceiling.

I can't believe that," he whispered.

"Your funeral."

Carty moved from the table to cross the room to the door. He stared out at the grasslands. He turned and looked at the man on the bunk.

"They'll be coming soon, searching."

He came back to the bunk and stood looking down at the man who lay there. "Morg finds you, he'll kill you. Or any of his boys. They got to get rid of you, way I look at it. Morg wants that ranch of yours."

"What kind of man is he?"

"He's a killer, a thief. He must've been planning this for a long time, ever since Kate wrote to him about getting married to you. He got her to come to him at Stovepipe. I think he maybe meant to bring her here himself, but there was that trouble with Bledsoe and Nogales Jack."

Carty explained how he and Ken Stevens had been friends, how Morgan Chance had tricked him into coming to Stovepipe, to make certain that Kate Chance would reach Macklin's ranch. Even as he spoke, a sullen rage filled his veins, that fury that the Kiowas termed the *ou'm ta'ta*, the blood anger. There was a need in him to kill.

Something of this Macklin sensed, for he licked his lips as he ran his eyes over this buckskin-shirted man with the low-hung gun and the long yellow hair. Carty's face was like brown granite in which blue eyes glowed. Macklin shivered. The man looked like a wolf, lean and dangerous.

Then Carty turned and smiled, and that inner passion seemed to fade. He came across the line cabin, walking with a swinging gait that reminded Peter Macklin more than ever of a hunting lobo.

"You're all right here. I got to get out, scout around."

Macklin nodded. He drew the blankets more closely around him, for he was shivering. He was surprised at that, for he was not cold. He would not want this man to be on his trail, following him. He had an idea that if he were, Amos Carty would find a way to kill him, very easily.

Carty walked out into the sunlight, caught up the rope on the grulla, saddled the blue horse, and rose up into the kak. He walked the horse off across the grasslands, and as he did he loosed his rifle in its scabbard.

His eyes never rested. They touched the hills behind him, traced them carefully, and then he brought his stare back to the grass. A man could be seen from far away on this grazeland, and discomfort was alive in him. He did not like to make a target like this, not at any time.

He reined the grulla northward, toward a series of breaks. These would shelter him, hide him from anything but a steady stare. He rode in among some mesquite and pinions, and after a time he pulled up to run his gaze across the land.

The land was empty, save for himself and some cattle.

Long after high noon he rode back to the cabin. Macklin was feverish, his eyes were overbright, and he would not eat. Carty watched him for a time, knowing that he would have to fetch a doctor.

He hesitated, because he did not like to leave Macklin alone and unprotected. The man who had gunned him down might be scouting around by now, trying to discover what was being done about the body he had left on the open range.

Still, Macklin needed medicines and a professional to look at that wound. He had done what he could, but he had the uneasy feeling that it was not enough.

Carty unsaddled the grulla and put the Cheyenne saddle on the pinto.

There was a town some twenty miles away. He had ridden through it some years back, when he had been drifting. Time had erased its name from his mind, but he knew where to find it. He rode away after a long look around him at the hills.

Sunset made a reddish blaze in the sky at his back as he cantered. The pinto was eager to run, but he held him in while he scanned the land around him. There was nothing but grass and hills, there was no sign of movement, and he wondered at that. A man like Pete Macklin ought to have folks out looking for him. His wife, at least. Or maybe somebody had told her lies.

It was dark when Carty reined in and looked at the town called Paydirt. He walked the pinto down the only street, eying the horses tied to the rail before the false-fronted saloon. One or two of them looked familiar. Carty reined in and ran his gaze over them. The more he looked, the more certain he was that he had seen those horses before.

There was a small hotel off to one side of a dry-goods store. He moved the pinto toward it, swung down, and went into the front room. There was a desk there, and a pretty girl behind it.

Carty took off his Plains hat. "There a doctor in this town, ma'am?"

She had brown hair and brown eyes, and skin that

showed the touch of the sun. She wore a gingham dress, very clean, but worn here and there from much usage.

"If you can call him that," she said tartly. "He's probably over in the saloon. He goes there every night." Her lips twisted into a bitter smile. "It's still early; he may not be dead drunk yet."

Carty nodded and turned away. He was going to have to go into that saloon and take away a drunk, sober him up, and get him out to that line cabin fit enough to do something to save a life. It might not be an easy task.

As he walked across the dirt road, he eased the leather thong off his Colt. His shoulders moved, and there was a cold restlessness inside him. Might be that he was walking toward his death, but a man had to do what he thought was needful.

With his left hand, he pushed open the batwings and then stepped sideways, waiting. Heads turned, he saw eyes widen in surprise, and he tensed.

Rawhide Bledsoe was there—or a man he took to be him—and at the table with him, those two men he had caught at that waterhole with Kate Chance. There were others like them at other tables. Looked like Bledsoe had brought his own little army with him. Well, he had known these men were in here; he had recognized their horses, or some of them.

"Girl at the hotel said there was a doctor here," Carty announced.

A lean man with gray in his hair stood away from the bar, faintly frowning. "I am Dr. Nolan. Francis Xavier Nolan."

"Man needs help. He was backshot."

"You do it?" asked Rawhide Bledsoe.

The smaller man beside Bledsoe put a hand on the other's arm.

"That's Amos Carty," said Lou Brent. "He never back-shot anybody. No need to."

Bledsoe murmured, "So you're the one."

The tall man in the spotted, black alpaca suit turned to look at Bledsoe. "Someone needs the attentions of a doctor, sir. The longer we spend here talking the more serious it may become."

"Hell with that."

Carty smiled faintly. "The doctor's right. You got something to say, or anything you want to do, you go ahead and do it. I'm waiting."

Rawhide Bledsoe felt Lou Brent tighten his grip on his gun arm.

"Easy, man. No sense in getting yourself killed. It ain't Carty you want, is it?"

Bledsoe ran his stare over the buckskin shirt, the dusty boots, the worn pants. He noted the cleanness of the shellbelt, the butt of the Colt ready to the hand. He also saw the blue eyes and their coldness, the readiness in them. Uneasiness came into his belly behind his belt buckle.

He growled, "He shot some of my men."

Carty said, "I'd do the same thing again, anybody comes after me with guns and tries to hurt a girl. That your speed, Bledsoe? Shooting down girls?"

There was an eagerness in that voice that Rawhide Bledsoe caught. He and his men might gun down this Carty, but something told him that by the time they did, he himself would be a dead man.

"I got a quarrel with her brother," Bledsoe snarled.

"He's here. Why don't you go find him?"

Waco Jimmy Blackwood asked softly, "Boss, you want us to do anything?"

Bledsoe waved a hand. "No need for that." He put his eyes on the man in buckskin. "You ride with Chance?"

"I ride by myself. Felt I owed him one, so I took his sister to that ranch. I learned I didn't owe him, so I came back. He owes me, now—and I mean to make him pay."

Bledsoe caught the muffled fury in that cold voice. He growled, "Morgan Chance belongs to me."

Carty smiled coldly, "Not any more. He's mine." He waited, then asked, "You ready, doctor? We got some riding to do."

The doctor walked across the floor, looking from one man to the other. He went past Carty out into the night. Carty took a backward step after him, and then another. When the batwings were at his back he stepped out onto the porch and sideways.

Rawhide Bledsoe said to Lou Brent, "You can let go now."

Brent shrugged and removed his hand. "Saved your life by doing that. You'd have gone for your gun, and you'd be dead if you had. Man, can't you recognize trouble when it stands there and dares you to tackle it?"

"I can use a gun."

"Sure, so can I. But that man there is hell almighty with a Colt. Got sort of a natural gift for it." Brent grinned. "I'd have loved to see him and Wild Bill hook up. Or Hardin. Nobody would see anything move until a dead man dropped. Or maybe two."

He rose and caught up Bledsoe's glass. "Hell, I'm thirsty. You too?"

Rawhide Bledsoe sat looking at his hands. Death had been standing there, looking at him tonight. Death had gone now, out into the night. Would take a little time before the warmth came back into his flesh. He needed that drink Brent was getting, he surely did.

When the smaller man returned, Bledsoe said, "You know, I forgot to ask him where I could find Morg Chance."

Little Lou chuckled. "That Carty will be around. You can ask him next time you see him. But by that time, Morg Chance may be buried."

Carty sat the saddle and waited while Dr. Nolan finished harnessing a pair of grays to a buckboard. When he was in the seat with the reins in his hands, Carty moved out ahead of him. He let the pinto set its own pace, and the wagon came trundling behind him. Overhead the stars were bright, and the few lights of town receded rapidly into the distance.

Carty glanced over his shoulder at the doctor.

"You sober enough?" he asked.

"Hadn't hardly started to drink."

There were no roads after they left the hard-packed dirt, swinging south and westward toward the line cabin. The buckboard jounced and bounced, and the creak of its rusted springs made a grating music to the ears. It annoyed Carty, that sound—it was audible to anyone within a mile or so who cared to listen. Carty liked to move as quietly as possible.

After a time he rode ahead of the buckboard and watched the land all around him. There was nobody else out here, nobody but that doctor and himself, far as he could tell. Carty caught the smell of sagebrush and felt a yearning to be riding free, away from here, out to the lonely hills.

If it hadn't been for Ken Stevens and that old friendship, he would be close to the Wyoming border by this time. He thought about his empty cabin and the little trails through the lodgepole pines and trembling aspens, and the sight of a big buck deer over his rifle sights. Something like homesickness tugged at him, but he put it aside; the hunting could wait. He had a different sort of hunting to do down here in the grasslands.

As soon as Pete Macklin was patched up and safe, he would ride out after Hobe Talbert and Morgan Chance. He knew where to find them.

The little line cabin was dark as they approached it.

Amos Carty reined in the pinto and said, "Better let me go ahead. Don't expect trouble, but you never know."

Dr. Nolan reined in his bays and sat there on the high seat, waiting. Carty swung down from the saddle and moved toward the cabin. His hand went to the door, lifted the latch, and pushed it.

The room was dark. He listened, but he could hear nothing, not even any breathing. For a moment he wondered if Peter Macklin had died.

He stepped inside and walked toward the bunk. Macklin lay there, and as he bent above him, he could catch his rasping breath. Carty stepped up to a crude table, scratched a match, and lighted a candle.

"You can come in now," he called.

The room was cold. Without waiting for the doctor, Carty went to the piled wood and the bucket of shavings and built a fire. In moments the shavings were blazing, the flames licking at the dried logs.

Dr. Nolan was working on Peter Macklin, opening his shirt, removing it, lifting out the blood-soaked grass with which Carty had stopped the flow of blood. He worked quietly, carefully. Carty watched him a moment, then eased out into the night darkness.

He unsaddled the pinto, staked it out, then caught up his Spencer rifle and strode off into the shadows. He hunkered down, waiting, his eyes always moving.

Carty was puzzled. Didn't seem right that no one had come searching for Macklin. When a man was missing on a ranch, there was a search. He could be hurt somewhere, with a broken leg or set on foot when his horse spooked and ran off. Could be that since his horse hadn't returned, they figured he was off somewhere, doing some sort of job.

Still, it didn't fit. Kate ought to be worried about him, if no one else was. That Kate Chance was a good girl, with a fine head on her shoulders. If she married a man, she would care for him; she wasn't the sort to let her husband get himself hurt and not do anything about it.

Maybe she couldn't. After all, Morg Chance and his men were at the Chessboard ranch. Hadn't been for that, Carty would have bet that Kate would have done some looking and brought the ranch hands with her.

A coyote sang its song to the moon, far off.

Carty rose up and began his walk. He moved half a mile out on the grasslands, pausing every so often to listen, to sniff at the wind. Buffalo Horn had taught him that trick. A touch of sweat, the smell of clothes worn too long, the scent of horseflesh, could sometimes be caught if a man were alert. There was nothing but the scent of sage and grass. He walked back to the cabin and into it.

Dr. Nolan was standing beside the bunk. He had been staring down at Macklin, now he turned to face Carty, and his face was grim.

"He's got a chance. Not much of a one, but he's still alive. I've cleaned out that wound, put medicine on it, front and back, and bandaged him. He'll need care. I'll come out to look at him tomorrow."

Carty shifted his weight, aware that he felt that an anchor had been tied around his leg. He was a man used to running with the wind, in whatever direction it might choose to blow. He did not accept shackles easily, and Peter Macklin was like a ball and chain to him right now.

He walked the doctor to his rig and watched him drive off.

He turned back into the cabin and stood looking down at Macklin. The man rested easier, his breathing more normal. Well, sleep would help him just as much as anything else. The blankets were pulled up around him; he seemed comfortable enough.

Carty found some jerky in his saddle pack and ate it.

Before he went to sleep he lifted out a shellbelt with a second Frontier-model Colt thrust into the worn holster and set about cleaning the gun. Been a long time since he had worn two guns, but even as he had stood in that Paydirt saloon he had told himself he could use another gun. Men like Bledsoe and Chance rode with other men at their backs, men who would join in any sort of gunfight. Might be a good idea to be prepared for them.

When he was satisfied with the Colt, he thrust it back into the holster, then looped the shellbelt about his middle. He adjusted it and felt his body begin to remember its weight, the tug at his left side. Satisfied, he nodded. Tomorrow he would ride off somewhere and practice using that left-hand gun.

Carty lifted his blanket and the Spencer rifle and went out into the night.

In the clear morning, he looked in on Macklin. The man was awake, his eyes were clear, and his lips twisted into a faint smile when he saw Carty.

"Doctor was here, wasn't he? Thought so. Bandaged up neat and proper. You get him?"

Carty nodded. He asked, "You hungry?"

Macklin shook his head, but Carty heated up the soup he had made, and sat down on the edge of the bunk. "Man's got to eat, he wants to get better."

He spoon-fed the man, gave him water from the little well back of the line cabin, then ate his own breakfast. His eyes went to Macklin again and again. The man was resting comfortably enough, but a line cabin was no place for a man to recover from a gunshot wound, not if he had better quarters to hold him.

"I'm riding to your ranch," Carty said at last. "Get a buckboard to haul you back. Be better if Kate comes out here to be with you." He chuckled. "She'll be a better nurse than me."

Macklin smiled weakly. "I'd appreciate it."

Carty hesitated. Suspicion was a natural part of him; he supposed it was because of his early training as a Kiowa. The Kiowas, like all Indians, had a lot of enemies: all white men, to their way of thinking, and most of all, other Indians. The Comanches were their friends—sometimes— and the Kiowa-Apache, for the most part. Everybody else was out to steal your goods or shoot you full of holes.

"Don't like to leave you alone," he said. "Not in the daytime, at least. Last night—well, you needed that doctor."

"I'll be all right. Nobody ever comes out here except one of the boys. If one of them shows up, I'll have him stay with me until you get back."

It would have to do, yet Carty was uneasy. Morgan Chance and his riders were somewhere around. He'd have bet those gold pieces Macklin had given him that Morg Chance was wondering where the hell Peter Macklin's dead body was. Carty could not believe that none of Chance's riders had ridden out to have a look at that body, especially since the bay Macklin had been riding had never returned. Carty's glance touched the lodgepole pine corral out back of the cabin. The bay was still there, and when it saw Carty, it nickered. There was grass in that crude corral, and water from a little stream that ran past it. The bay, along with his own pinto, would be all right until he got back here with Kate.

He saddled the grulla and mounted. It would take him some time to get to the ranch. He was no fool to go riding out there in plain sight for somebody to have at him with a Winchester or a Henry rifle. It might take some doing, that, to come down on that ranch house without being seen by anybody but Kate Macklin.

The sun was high; it made sweat streaks along the middle of his back, and he tilted the flat-crowned Plains hat lower to hide the glare from his eyes as he rode. Under its brim his eyes were watchful. He saw the grass bend as a breeze tipped it. He noted the flight of a grouse startled by his passage. Up there in the hills there would be deer or bighorns, maybe even an elk. Been a while since he had feasted on elk meat.

Once he got shet of Peter Macklin, he might—

Something moved, off to the south. Instantly Carty was out of the saddle, tugging at the grulla. He had trained this horse; it rolled over for him and lay there motionless so the tall grasses would hide it.

Carty slid the Spencer forward.

Might be one of Morg's boys coming this far west to hunt Macklin and his bay. Carty lifted off the Plains hat and raised his head to take a look. Nobody would see the top of his head at a distance, not if he didn't move.

The rider was coming closer. He was not riding fast; he turned one way and then another, and Carty realized he was searching the grasslands. And he was coming straight for Carty. When the rider came closer, Carty let his lips twitch into a grin.

The rider was Kate Macklin.

Carty was about to rise up and call to her when he heard the sound—it was distant, something like eight or ten miles away, but he heard it. And he froze, still crouched in the grass.

Gunshots. Not just one, but several.

Who would be shooting behind him? And at what?

Coldness ran down his spine. Peter Macklin was back there, where the shots had come from.

CHAPTER 9

Carty stood up, lifting his Plains hat and waving with it.

Kate Macklin saw him, reined her spotted pony around, and came trotting toward him. She wore a shirt and a riding outfit, and she carried a quirt in her right hand. Her long brown hair blew free under her hat.

Were those tears on her cheeks?

She came up to him and stared down at him, and now Carty knew them for tears. There was fright in this girl, so strong he could almost smell it. Her gloved hands were trembling as they held the reins.

"What are you doing here?" she asked. "I thought you'd ridden away."

"Came back."

She eyed him thoughtfully. "Any special reason?"

"Found out something about your brother."

She considered that, head tilted. "And what did you learn about my brother?"

"That he set me up. And that he was coming here."

She nodded. "I don't know anything about what he did to you, but he came here. He's at the ranch now."

Carty turned away, saying, "He have his men with him?"

"Why, no. He came by himself."

The grulla had risen and was standing, waiting. Carty shoved the rifle into its scabbard and lifted it into the kak. He caught up the reins and swung the grulla to the west.

"He didn't come alone. He came with his boys. I saw them near the Little Colorado."

"And I tell you, he came alone to the ranch."

"Sure he did. But his boys are around. One of them shot your husband."

Kate Macklin swayed in the saddle, her face white. "Shot him?"

Carty eyed her. "Why'd you think he hadn't come home? Or didn't you care?"

The girl stiffened. Fury brightened her eyes, and she half-raised the quirt as though to lash out at him.

"Found him two days ago, shot down from behind and bleeding to death. Did what I could, and got a doctor from Paydirt." He paused, then asked, "You hear those gunshots just now?"

She shook her head, touching her lips with her tongue.

"No. No, I didn't."

"Just pray that your brother's boys didn't find that line cabin. Well? You want to see him or don't you?"

"You're insufferable."

"Maybe so, but you want to put eyes on that husband of yours, you'd better ride. He isn't in good shape, not at all."

He set the pace, letting the grulla run. The spotted pony kept even with him, and when he glanced sideways at the girl, he saw her face white and tense, with faint shadows under her eyes.

After a time, Carty said, "Thought you might be suspicious of Morg, his showing up right after your wedding."

"He told me he had enemies, that he had to avoid them."

"He's got one more enemy, right now."

"Who is that?"

"He had a friend of mine gunned down so I'd ride to Stovepipe and bring you here."

"I don't believe it!"

His shoulders moved in a casual shrug. "Don't matter to me what you believe. I'm telling you I'd never have showed up in Stovepipe to play nursemaid to you if Ken Stevens were still alive. Morg had him shot down by Pike Shattuck and two other men. I want to see Morg about that. Ken Stevens was my friend."

Kate Chance rode easily beside him as he let the grulla set an even pace. Her glances touched his face and found it hard, relentless. This man might not be an Indian, but he thought as Indians did, she sensed. There was pride in him, and a righteous anger.

He disturbed her. He was unlike any other man she had ever met. She noted that he did not ride off across the grasslands but angled their run toward the low hills. From moment to moment he rose to stand in the stirrups and run his stare all around them. Coldness touched her spine.

She found her voice after a frightened moment. "Do you think someone will try to harm us? Here, on the ranch?"

His eyes touched her. They were withdrawn, almost icy. "You surprised? If they could get rid of you too, it sure would help your brother."

Shock numbed her. "I—I don't understand."

Carty led the way into a wash and along it for a time, then came up onto some high ground where they would be sheltered by box elders and willows. He reined in here, always staring out across the flatlands.

"You're the most suspicious man," she flared. "What are you looking for?"

"The men who did that shooting. If they're headed this way, I'd rather not have them see us."

Kate shook her head; she just did not understand this man. "Do you really think those men would shoot me?"

His smile was hard. "Be smart if they did. Then nobody would contest Morg in his plan to take over the ranch."

"You're insufferable."

He made no reply to that; he went on looking out across the land, and after a time he toed the grulla to a walk. She followed after him, scowling angrily at his buckskinned back. There was something about this Amos Carty that roused her temper, but she had to admit that she felt perfectly safe with him. She could not imagine anything frightening him or taking him by surprise.

"Are you always ready for trouble?" she muttered.

"Safest way."

She followed the grulla among the trees, along the pine-needled slopes, among ponderosa pine and junipers. It was cool here under the trees, the hot glare of the sun was shadowed, and the hooves of their horses made scarcely any sound. They went like shadows among the tree boles until they came at last to a meadow that ran its grasses out onto the grazeland.

"Cabin's yonder, behind those trees," he announced.

She waited beside him, letting him look. Her own eyes regarded him, seeing his leanness, his readiness, the constant activity of his eyes. The flat-crowned Plains hat hid most of his face in shadow, but his eyes gleamed almost like those of a wild animal.

He drew the Spencer rifle from its scabbard and held it across the pommel of his saddle. "All right. Seems safe enough. We can go now."

He rode off ahead of her, and she followed almost in his tracks. She saw the line of trees in the distance, and after a time the shape of the line cabin with the fenced corral behind it.

Carty did not ride directly toward the cabin; he came in on it from an angle, and his right hand held the rifle ready. After a time he walked the grulla forward, right at the cabin. He leaned from the saddle and searched the ground carefully.

When he tensed, Kate asked, "What is it?"

"Three men were here."

She stared at him. "How can you know that?"

"Horses' tracks. Three different horses." He stared southward. "They went away from here fast, at a gallop." He turned his head and looked at the line cabin. "Must have been them shooting."

Kate swung from the saddle. "If Peter is in that cabin, I'm going to him."

"Wouldn't, if I were you. He may not be nice to look at."

She swung around. "Wha—what do you mean?"

"Those gunshots I heard. Remember? Looks to me as if your brother's boys found your husband."

He came to the ground, still with the rifle, and he walked past her toward the cabin door. With the muzzle of the rifle, he pushed at the door. It opened inward. For an instant he stood there, then went inside.

Almost instantly he was at the door again. "You'd better not come in."

Fear ran deep inside Kate Chance, and she felt her knees quiver. But she knew she had to go inside that cabin. She took a step and then another, aware of his eyes on her. She did not know that her face was white, that her eyes were hollowed and frightened.

Carty stepped aside, almost reluctantly.

"He didn't have a chance," he whispered.

She darted her eyes at him, then looked straight ahead as she went into the cabin. For a moment, she froze.

He lay as though asleep, with the blankets pulled up over him. But even in the indistinct light, she could see the holes in the blankets where the bullets had gone. There was a grouping of half a dozen bullets. . . .

She swayed, and Carty was beside her, his arm about her middle, turning her, leading her outside the cabin. He made her walk for a little time, until the blood came back into her face.

"He was—such a good man," she whispered, and then: "It's all my fault. If I hadn't agreed to marry him, he'd be alive today."

She began to cry in wracking sobs that shook her body in spasms. Carty held her against him, let the tears come and the agonized moans. After a time she straightened, sought for a handkerchief, wiped her wet cheeks, and dried her eyes.

She whispered, "You must know who killed him."

"Got me an idea."

Her tear-wet eyes lifted, and Carty was surprised by the sudden hardness in them. "You find his killers, Amos. You go find them and kill them. I'll pay you a thousand dollars for each man."

"That's killer's pay, and I don't kill for money."

"For what, then?"

"I owe three men already. If they're the same ones who killed Ken Stevens, I'll take care of them."

She caught his hand and clung to it. "Come to the ranch. I can hire you, can't I? To—to help me?"

"First thing you'd better do is get a buckboard here, take your husband's body back, and bury it."

Kate stared at the line cabin, eyes wide. "Ought we just —leave him here? Like that?"

"I'll close the door. Then we'll ride."

Carty took her northward into the hills, through a series of small canyons and ravines where the ball cholla and beaver tail cactus made a panorama of white and gold against the barren soil. Kate rode easily, saying nothing, content within herself to follow where this man took her. There was a sorrow in her; tears came to her eyes from time to time, yet there was also a strange serenity within her as well.

Once, when Carty reined in at the top of a cactus-studded ridge, she let her lips twist into a weak smile. "You're the most cautious man I've ever seen. If I didn't know better, I'd think you were afraid."

"I am afraid. I got me two gangs to think on: your brother's men, and those who ride with Rawhide Bledsoe."

"The man who tried to stop us from reaching the ranch? But that's over and done with."

"Is it? Then what's Bledsoe doing in Paydirt?"

"I—I didn't know."

"No more than you know your brother brought his gunhands with him. They didn't ride with him just to keep him from getting lonesome. Morg's got himself a plan."

She eyed him carefully. "What sort of plan?"

Carty brought his stare from the land below him to the girl. The grulla shifted under him, he swayed easily in the saddle, but she noted that his hands were always on that rifle he carried across the saddlehorn, and she felt instinctively that he was ready to use it at any moment.

"You're a widow, now," he said softly. "You got yourself a nice ranch, with plenty of cattle. A good holding. Morg knows that. Morg moves in on you. Pretty soon, Morg takes over." Carty shrugged. "He may let you live, you don't make him any trouble. You do, and you may get yourself shot, same way your husband did."

"That's incredible!"

Carty shrugged. "You asked. I told you."

"But I cannot believe Morgan would act that way against me," she muttered weakly.

"Why not? You somebody special?"

Her eyes locked with his, and she read hard truth inside them. This man had no iron in the fire, he stood to gain nothing, one way or the other, by what happened between Morgan and herself. She sank back against the saddle cantle and felt weakness move in her.

"What you're saying is, my own brother rode down here into Arizona Territory to rob my husband and me to take over our ranch."

"About the size of it."

Kate shivered. Belief came hard to her, but the more she thought of what Carty was telling her, the more she felt compelled to admit he might be right. What other reason was there for Peter to have been gunned down and left dead in that line cabin?

Almost unconsciously, she put out her hand and gripped his arm. "You won't leave me, will you? If you do . . ."

Again that coldness settled inside her, and the beginning of panic, of terror. She knew little about her half brother, but what little she did was not reassuring. That ride she and Carty had taken to reach Chessboard was proof enough that Morgan had enemies; moreover, someone had killed Peter. Only her half brother stood to profit from that.

Her fingers tightened on his arm. Carty nodded at her, not smiling. "I'll stay around, for a time. But I do things my way. I ride alone, I pick and choose the men I feel must die."

He paused a moment. "That includes your brother."

Carty saw the shock in her eyes. She touched her lips

with a nervous tongue. "Yes. I can see that. I mustn't hobble you."

Her hand fell away. Carty jerked the reins in his left hand, and the grulla began its walk. Kate followed him, frowning and thoughtful. She had only one friend in this country: Carty. Everyone else, with the possible exception of her ranch hands, were her enemies, or to be treated as such until she could learn the truth.

Carty brought her through the high hills, among the mesquite and the tall saguaro cactus, until they could see the ranch house lying placid in the sunlight. There was no activity below; the buildings seemed empty and abandoned. Yet there were horses in the corrals.

"Looks safe enough," Carty nodded. "You can go on down, now."

She glanced at him. "And you? What will you be doing?"

He smiled thinly. "Got me a trail to follow."

She could get nothing more out of him, she knew, so she reined her bay around and trotted past him. Once she turned, to see him standing there behind a sheltering Joshua tree, his gaze fixed on her. She rode more confidently after that, knowing he was watching. Guarding her. It made a warm feeling inside her, where it had been so cold.

As she cantered into the ranch yard, the house door opened and her brother came out, looking at her inquiringly. There was an ease in Morgan Chance, a confidence, which she saw now for the first time.

"You been gone a spell," he said.

"I—found Peter," she made herself say.

He came down off the porch and walked to her, watching her carefully. "Where was he? Why didn't he come back?"

"He couldn't. He was dead."

He never even blinked, she noticed. It was no news to him. She said, "He was in that line cabin, shot full of holes."

"The line cabin?" he blurted.

He had made a mistake. His face showed signs of the surprise in him, but it smoothed out and became solicitous. If she had not been warned by Amos Carty, she would never have noticed that blurring of his features. In that moment, her heart hardened against her half brother.

Kate swung down from the saddle and began to walk the bay toward the corral. Her half brother fell into step beside her, eying her warily.

"You say somebody shot him?"

"I do. They stood over him while he was helpless in a bunk and they made sure he was dead." Her eyes touched his face. "I'll have to go bring his body in for burial. Where are the boys?"

Morgan Chance shrugged. "Out on the range. No need to bother about them. I can take care of it. You stay here."

"No, Morgan. I am coming along. And I will have the boys ride with me."

His eyes were scanning her face, seeking to discover blame on her features. But she kept her facial muscles under control, she met his stare casually, and any suspicion in him dropped away.

He reached for the reins. "Let me do that for you. You have enough on your mind right now."

She let him take the bay; she stood and watched him walk away. If it had not been for Carty, for the knowledge that he was out there somewhere, she would have broken down. Even so, tears were in her eyes, and she turned her head away so that Morgan would not notice.

Carty rode through the late-afternoon hours, back toward the line cabin. He was in no hurry; the men he was after would not suspect he was coming for them. They would be taking their time, they might even be looking for a place to camp, to spend the night.

He let the grulla set its own pace. He came back to the line cabin, and then he put the grulla to a circular walk until he picked up the trail of those three horses. He studied them more carefully when he came upon them, so that he would impress them in his memory.

Then he rode after them, cantering, bending from time to time in the saddle to scan the grasslands, to make certain it was their trail he followed. They were riding without a thought in the world about their own safety. None of them drew up to scan their back trail. He doubted even that they turned in their saddles to look back the way they had come.

He smiled grimly.

Even after the sun sank behind the Santa Marias, Carty kept riding. It was only when the sky darkened so that he could no longer read the sign he followed that he swung from the saddle and made a little fire on which to cook the big jackrabbit he had shot. He cooked his meal and ate it, then put out the fire and swung back into the saddle. He walked the grulla for two miles before he unsaddled and wrapped himself in his blanket.

Toward midmorning of the next day, he drew up, sitting the saddle and staring at the hoofprints in puzzlement. The men he was following were heading for Chessboard ranch, cutting eastward and riding fast.

Carty paused to build himself a smoke, staring at those tracks and considering what they told him. The men would not be going to the ranch unless they were sure of a friendly reception. Morg would welcome them, he would take them on as ranch hands, they would be given a place to sleep in the bunkhouse.

Slowly, little by little, Morg was building his own ranch.

Where did that leave Kate?

Carty followed their trail, easing along. He was in no hurry; those men wouldn't be leaving the country. They would be at Chessboard whenever he wanted them. Yet he had to make sure.

He circled around and came down on the ranch from the north, from the high hills. He dismounted, pulled the grulla to the ground, and lay down himself, behind a big boulder, and used his eyes.

There were men at the ranch, moving about between the house and the corrals. He saw no sign of Kate. Had they buried Macklin? Was that his grave marker, that wooden cross he could barely make out on the grassy slope half a mile from the buildings?

After a time, he saw a man bring a saddled horse from the corral, and even at this distance he recognized it as the bay that Kate had ridden yesterday. Kate came out then, mounted up, and began to ride away. Carty followed her with his eyes. She was heading for the hills.

He waited for half an hour, to make certain that no one was following her. Then he rose and stepped into the kak and rode off on a tangent that would bring him close to Kate and her bay in about an hour.

She was in the foothills when he came down on her, and once again, she had been crying. She reined in at first sight of him and waited, brushing at her tears with the heel of her hand.

"You had visitors," Carty said. "The three men I've been following."

She nodded. "They rode in this morning. One was the man called Shattuck. The others—I'm not sure about their names. One was tall and lean, with a cast in one eye—"

"Ed Wells."

"—and the third was called Hobe."

"Hobe Talbert. Figures."

She eyed him. "I just couldn't stay there any longer." There was appeal in her frightened eyes. "I hoped I'd meet you, or that you would find me."

Carty felt irritation. He wanted no woman riding beside him on the trail he was taking. A woman would slow him down, make herself conspicuous when he wanted to hide.

"Fort Apache, that's where I'll take you."

Kate stiffened. "No. I won't leave this ranch land. It's mine, Amos. I won't let my brother drive me out."

He shifted comfortably in the kak, trying to muster up arguments in his mind so he could put them on his tongue. He was aware of her bright brown eyes watching him, almost as though she knew what he was planning.

"I'm safer with you than anywhere else," she said gently. A moment later, she added, "Please?"

"Won't be easy," he muttered.

She nodded solemnly. "I know that. I came prepared for trouble."

His eyes went over her. "Didn't bring much."

She smiled. "There are blankets in that line cabin. I shall take one. And as for food, I shall eat what you eat. No more."

Carty told himself he was a plain damn fool. But he said it under his breath and without moving his lips. Had Kate Macklin been a Kiowa girl, now—well, that wouldn't have been so bad. A Kiowa female would know how to handle herself in what was coming. This one was putting it all up to him.

"No sense standing here," he muttered. "Let's go get that blanket."

They came down on the line cabin during the late afternoon. Carty would not permit her to dismount; he went alone into the cabin and caught up two blankets and a couple of cans of tomatoes. From a gunnysack, he made a pack and carted what he had taken out to the grulla.

He went to the little corral behind the cabin, where the pinto stood with Macklin's black, fashioned hackamores from Macklin's lariat, and led the horses out after him. Swinging into the kak, he walked with Kate beside him out across the edge of the grass until he could turn up into the hills.

Carty made a tiny camp in among the tumbled rocks and prickly pear, giving Kate a can of the tomatoes and some jerky, keeping one for himself, and finishing what was left of the jerky. They did not speak; there was nothing for them to say, Carty felt.

He thought, though. He probed his mind for the best place to keep Kate Macklin while he went out after those men. He could not take her with him; it was out of the question. He wished he could keep her in that line cabin, but she would be unprotected there, prey to Morg's killers.

There was Bledsoe to consider, too. Bledsoe would be pleased to get his hands on Kate, use her to force Morg out into the open. If Morg didn't respond to that threat— as Carty was sure he would not—then Bledsoe would turn her over to his own riders, for sport.

Carty shifted uncomfortably. He could find no answers.

It took him a time to fall asleep. The fire was out; they

were safe enough, with Kate back there under a juniper's branches. Nobody could come at them with the horses picketed here and there. The trouble was, he could do nothing with the girl along. He felt like a horse with a hobble.

He slept. Dimly he was aware of the night sounds, of the whisper of wind through the branches of the spruce trees, the distant wail of a coyote, the utter stillness that lay upon the land. He slept more heavily now, but a part of him was waiting for any danger that might come upon him in the darkness.

At dawn he was up, making a little fire, putting his coffee pot on it. He had no food—he would have to hunt today to keep Kate fed. Himself, he could go without food for a long time, but he had the girl to feed.

He was moving toward the horses when he heard the faint click of a horseshoe on stone.

CHAPTER 10

Carty went off his feet in a dive, his hands going for his Colts. He landed on a knee, rolled over with his six-guns in his hands, and lay on his belly behind a clump of prickly pear. Its broad pads hid him almost completely.

There was no one around. Kate still lay sleeping, off to one side. He waited, head up, listening.

There was a man near here—at the very least, a horse. And Carty was suspicious enough to know that where there was a horse, there was an enemy. He lay breathing easily, waiting.

"Got you covered, Carty," a voice called, with humor in it.

His hands tightened their hold on his gunbutts. No need to talk; he had nothing to say to men who came up on him in the first dawn light, so silently. All he asked was a target to put a bullet into.

A man rode into view from between a tall saguaro and a smaller devil's-claw, and off to one side of him another, and then another. They had rifles in their hands, searching the ground for him, and there was a confidence in them that he mistrusted.

They would not come at him so openly unless they were sure they had him. Uneasily he turned, stared around him, at the higher ground, at the rocks off to one side. He saw nothing but barren ground and the plants that grew in this dry soil.

He turned back to the three riders. He knew them for men who rode with Bledsoe, but he could put a name only to one of them: Waco Jimmy Blackwood. Blackwood was a drifter, a gunhand who had ridden with Clay Allison. He had faced him down in that little sink where they had taken Kate Chance, but the situation was reversed here. Waco Jimmy would not be so confident unless—

The click of a gunhammer being drawn back warned him.

Carty whirled and saw three men rising up from behind some boulders. They had guns in their hands, aimed at him. He fired, thumbing his hammers as fast as was possible.

Even as he shot, even as he saw one man go down and then another, fire burned across his hip. Something drove him sideways, like a great weight on his shoulder. Then his skull exploded.

He opened his eyes on darkness.

For a moment, he thought he had been blinded, but he saw moonlight on rocks and the cholla pads off to one side. Pain lanced through him, and as he tried to rise, he fell back. Mouth open, he sobbed at the air, drawing it into his lungs.

He was shot up, he knew that. He might die, here under the Arizona moonlight. But he was not dead yet. Not yet!

He crawled, just a little—enough to know that he was going to die out here, shot full of holes and bleeding so badly, unless he could get to water and a place to hide out until he could doctor himself. There were plants a man could use on wounds, chewing them until they formed a sort of paste, clapping them over the bullet-holes.

Carty did not think he could find those plants—not before he died. His lips twisted in a faint grin. At least he wasn't dead yet.

He went on crawling.

He came to a little stream sometime after nightfall, but he could hear the trickling water, and it sent new strength into his weakened body. He had come on some chokecherry, had torn up the roots and chewed them as he crawled. He spat out those roots and held them in a hand when he came up to the stream.

Carty drank sparingly, enough to put new life into him.

Then he stripped off his clothes, laboriously, and looked down at his blood-covered body. He had taken one across the hip, and another bullet in his side. Neither one was enough to kill him, he guessed, once he could stop that bleeding and get himself a rest.

He put the chewed chokecherry roots on the wounds and lay there naked in the shade of a saguaro, close to the stream. He slept.

At dawn he woke to drink, to check his wounds. The chewed chokecherry roots had stopped the bleeding, but his body was painful. It hurt to move. Indianlike, he lay back, patient and waiting. Hunger disturbed him, but he had been hungry before, at other times in his life.

Right now he needed strength and that water.

He put all thoughts of Kate Macklin out of his head—as much as he could, anyhow. He could do nothing to help her, barely enough to help himself. But he thought about her and about the men who had taken her.

For three days he lay beside that stream, letting his wounds heal and his strength come back, such as it was. On the morning of the fourth day he fashioned a trap of thongs he tore from his buckskin shirt, and where he had seen the big horseshoe hares come to drink, he set it carefully.

That night he ate everything of a hare but its bones and skin. He reset the trap and ate again, in the first pale light of morning. After that he began to walk around. There was no hurry in him. Bledsoe and his men would be there when he came for them. So would Morg Chance.

Besides, he needed guns and a horse.

The men who had shot him had taken his Colts and the grulla. They had everything of his except the clothes he wore and his shellbelts that were still buckled about his hips. It felt odd, the lack of weight where his six-guns normally hung. Well, he would do something abut that too, when the time came.

But not yet. Not yet awhile.

For the next week he haunted the high hills, moving around every day to gain strength, returning to the site of the ambush, studying the tracks. Bledsoe had split his party; Waco Jimmy and the two men with him had shown themselves, while the others had circled around behind him.

Carty smiled coldly. Had he been alone, they would never have found him. Came of being saddled with a woman. He had let the fire burn on too long because the air had been cold and Kate had been shivering. The girl was gone, now. Nobody to protect but himself.

First thing he needed was a gun. Or maybe a horse.

He gave some thought to his wants. After a time he chuckled softly and began his walk. Anger built in him the longer he moved downward off the hills and toward the grasslands. His moccasins had been on the grulla. He would have liked to be walking in moccasins right now instead of these boots with the high heels. High heels were fine when a man was riding; they kept his feet from slipping through the stirrups. But they were pure torture when they were used for footwork. Stoically, as enigmatic as any Kiowa, he ignored the pains of his feet and went on striding.

He came up to the line cabin in the moonlight.

He opened a can of tomatoes and ate the fruit, sitting on the edge of a bunk. Then he stretched out on the bunk and fell asleep.

The next day he walked across the grasslands, heading toward Chessboard. He was halfway there when two riders came into view, saw him, and moved toward him. He recognized them as Billy Andrews and the flat-faced man who'd said his name was Poke Drummond.

Drummond reined in and grinned faintly.

"Looks like you bought trouble."

Carty nodded. "Give me a leg up. I have news for Morg."

Drummond kicked a foot free of the stirrup and braced himself as Carty lifted up behind the saddle.

The flat-faced man said, "We been hunting for the girl."

"Figured that. Bledsoe's got her."

Drummond touched his horse with a toe. "You with her at the time?"

"Got me a couple of his boys. Not enough. They were all around me."

"I saw the bulletholes in your jacket."

Billy Andrews exalimed, "They must've shot you up pretty hard."

"Bad enough. They took my horse and my guns. They made a mistake."

Billy Andrews eyed him. "What kind of mistake?"

"They should have killed me."

Something in his voice made young Billy shiver.

They rode into the ranch yard with Morgan Chance standing there and watching them. There was suspicion in the stare he put on Carty and Carty swung down before him.

"Thought you were off somewhere in Colorado," he growled.

"Started off there, Morg. Got sidetracked. Came back here to think about an offer Macklin made to me. I could use some money right now. Where is he?"

Morgan Chance eyed this lean man warily. Those eyes that stared back at him held not the slightest flicker of emotion. Wounded he might have been—or maybe still was—but he was like a wild animal, motionless, wary, ready to jump one way or another at the slightest hint.

"He's dead," Morg said softly.

Carty nodded. "Must have been Bledsoe or his boys."

He saw the sudden relief in Morgan Chance's eyes and fought back the inclination to smile. He said, "I met up with Kate some days ago, she seemed upset, so I rode along with her, just to keep an eye on her."

He had Morg's attention now. Had it good. He shrugged. "Wasn't too much good, at that. Bledsoe and his boys caught me in a bind." Carty shook his head. "It was at dawn; I'd just waked up and they were all around me. I got as many of them as I could before they put lead in me and left me for dead."

He added softly, "I owe them, Morg."

Morg Chance shivered. He said, "I'll do anything to help, Amos."

"Guns. A horse."

"Easy enough."

Carty smiled faintly. "And food. Seems I haven't eaten anything but half-cooked rabbit for the past month."

They ate steak that night, and sliced potatoes with onions. Carty ate in the bunkhouse with the hands. Across from him he saw Hobe Talbert with Pike Shattuck beside him, and a little farther down the big table, Ed Wells. There was amusement in their eyes as they regarded him, and Carty told himself that if Bledsoe's men hadn't put lead in him, these three might have done it.

Carty said little, as was his custom, but he used his eyes. He saw the clannishness of the Chessboard riders, who shied away from Talbert and the others. In a little while, he told himself, Morg would give the Chessboard men their walking papers and then bring in the rest of his own crowd.

Morgan Chance had a good thing going here.

When he was done eating he walked across to the ranch house. Morg called to him to enter.

Morg was stretched out in that morris chair that had belonged to Peter Macklin. He had one of Macklin's cigars lighted and was puffing smoke lazily, appreciatively. His hand gestured Carty to a chair.

"You going after Bledsoe and his men?" Morg asked.

"Figure I owe them. Wouldn't you?"

Chance nodded heavily. There was amusement in him, same as there had been in Talbert and the other two. Morg was figuring that Amos Carty would do his job for him, get rid of the only men Morgan Chance had to fear.

"Got some guns you might as well take. Belonged to Kate's husband."

Chance rose, moved across the room, and opened a drawer. He lifted out two Patterson Colts, long-barreled, with walnut buttplates. He held them a moment, frowning.

"They look like good guns, but there's something wrong with their grips. Just don't suit me. You take 'em."

He put the guns down on the table and watched as Carty rose and moved toward him. Morgan Chance had never known a man who walked and moved the way Amos Carty did, so easily, like a cat gliding along. Carty put his hands on the guns, frowned a moment, then hefted them.

"They'll do," he said quietly, and slid them into his holsters.

Morg grinned. "Now you'll need a rifle. Got a whole mess of those, over on the wall, in a rack made out of solid mahogany. Quite a gunrack, this one."

Carty admired it, as he was meant to do, but he was more interested in the rifles than in the rack that held them. There was a Sharps buffalo gun, two Henrys, and a new Winchester. He reached for the Winchester.

"Never had me a gun like this," he muttered, turning it over and over. "Looks like it's hardly ever been used."

"Brand-new. Macklin told me—when I came here, that first night—that it had just arrived. He'd never even used it, poor devil."

His sorrow rang false to Carty; there was gloating in that voice, in the eyes that touched Carty, then fell away. He could afford to give away guns; he was getting the ranch and safety in return, if Carty got Bledsoe off his trail.

"Obliged, Morg," Carty said softly.

Morgan Chance waved a hand. "A horse, too. You'll need a good one. Pick out the one you want first thing to-morrow. Anything that has hooves, you can have."

Carty nodded. "I'll be going, then. Got to bed down now if I'm to be up early enough to go find those men."

"There are empty bunks at the bunkhouse."

"Not for me. I'll sleep on the ground."

Chance grinned. "Still the Indian."

"Gets to be a habit."

He walked out into the sunlight with Morgan Chance behind him, framed against the ranch house light in the doorway, watching him. Carty moved toward the bunkhouse, pausing only long enough to lift up a blanket and nod his head at the men busy over a poker game, then walked off into the hills.

Pike Shattuck watched him go, hands wrapped around his cards. "That Indian always makes me a mite uneasy," he said to the room.

Hobe Talbert cursed and reached for the toothpicks they were using as chips. "He ain't human. He's like the wind—comes one way and then another, and nobody's ever quite sure when he's liable to blow up into a storm."

Poke Drummond chuckled. "Good man to walk around."

Young Billy Anderson said eagerly, "I'd like to go talk to him."

"Don't do it, kid. Liable to get yourself shot—even," Drummond added, "if you could find him."

Carty was at the corral when the Chessboard riders came out into the early light, sitting on the top pole and studying the horses. Drummond walked over to him and put his elbows on the pole near him.

"That black has a nice gait," he murmured.

"Wouldn't last two days in the hills."

Drummond smiled faintly. "That may be so. What one do you fancy?"

"The dun."

Poke Drummond showed surprise. "He's only half broke."

"So am I. We'll get along. Whose horse is he?"

"Nobody's. Too cantankerous."

Drummond watched as Carty lifted a rope and walked

toward the dun. The big horse eyed him warily, stepping sideways. Very faintly, Drummond could hear Carty talking but could not make out the words. To his surprise, the dun pricked up its ears at the sound of that voice and seemed to lose a little of his nervousness. Carty slid the rope around his neck, led him toward the gate, and brought him out into the yard.

He chose a worn Pueblo saddle and slung it over the dun's back. The horse arched its back, but Carty spoke to it, and after a moment, slid on a bridle.

Drummond said, "You made that look easy. I've tried to saddle that horse and gave it up as a bad job."

"Didn't know the right words."

"What words are those?"

Carty chuckled. "Kiowa. This one was an Indian pony at one time."

He ran his hand along the smooth, muscular quarter. "See this? That's an Indian brand, made with milkweed juice."

Drummond craned his neck. "Be damned. Never saw that before."

The dun bucked a little as Carty stepped into the saddle, but quieted down after a time and seemed content. Carty walked him to the bunkhouse hitchrail and tied the reins. He swung down into an aroma of cooking beef.

After he had eaten, he moved out into the ranch yard and swung up on the dun. The Winchester was in the scabbard, and the Patterson Colts were in his holsters. He fought down an impulse to smile at the thought of those handguns. If Morg had traded hands, now . . .

He saw Morgan Chance emerge from the ranch house and angle his walk toward him. Carty walked the dun to meet him.

"I'll be riding, Morg. And—thanks."

Morgan Chance shrugged. "You're doing me a favor, Indian. I appreciate that."

"Just aiming to get my own back."

He waited, but Morgan Chance said nothing about his sister, so Carty asked. "What you want me to do about Kate, if I find her?"

"Bring her back, of course."

Morgan Chance said those words, but he did not mean them. The lie was there in his eyes, easy to read. If his sister were dead, he would be a happy man. This Chessboard ranch would be his then.

Carty wondered if Peter Macklin had any living relatives. Even if he did, even if they learned what had happened, Morgan Chance could strip Chessboard, drive its cattle northward into Nevada, Utah, or Colorado, maybe even into Wyoming, and set up for himself. It was a smart way of robbing a man.

The thought touched him that once he had rid Morgan Chance of Rawhide Bledsoe, Morg might send men after him to quiet his tongue. Carty felt anger touch him as he stared down into Chance's face. One of these days he would have to kill Morgan Chance.

He rode away from Chessboard without a backward glance. The dun had an easy gait, a long stride. It was a good horse, might even be the equal of his grulla. He meant to get that grulla back, soon as he'd found out about Kate.

He rode across the grasslands without troubling to hide himself. He was safe enough here. Chance would not send Pike Shattuck or Hobe Talbert after him, not until he learned what had happened to Kate. All he had to be wary of were Rawhide Bledsoe and his men.

But they would not be on Chessboard land—not in any force, anyhow.

Toward midafternon he came on the campsite where he had been shot. Without leaving the saddle, he studied the ground, memorizing the hoofmarks of the horses. There had been seven of them, all told. Two of those men he had killed before going down before the others' bullets.

They had carried the dead bodies off with them, along with Kate. He made out the prints of the grulla, too. They were headed southward, toward that little town of Paydirt.

Their trail was easy to follow. Carty gave it only a small part of his attention as he rode. He was more interested in what he might discover about Kate Macklin. He did not believe Bledsoe would harm her; she was too important to him alive. Bledsoe wanted revenge on Morgan Chance, not on his sister. At the same time, she would be well guarded.

When he came to a line of foothills, he moved in among the Douglas fir and the ponderosa pine. He swung from the saddle and lifted out the Patterson Colts. A slow smile touched his lips. These guns had been specially crafted, one made for the left hand, and one for the right.

He switched them and let his big hands settle around the butts.

They felt natural to him this way.

He remembered the way Morg Chance had scowled at them when he had picked them up. He had frowned himself when he had first touched them. Almost instantly, he had realized the truth. Guns such as these were not easily come by.

He dropped them into the holsters and tensed.

His hands flashed and lifted. Flame spat from the muzzles of the guns, and two blossoms on a juniper leaped through the air. Carty nodded, satisfied. His hands were not used to these Pattersons as yet, but they would be.

Again and again he drew, holstered them, and drew again.

He did not fire them, however. He had done that once, to test their accuracy. Satisfied as to that, he needed only to familiarize himself with their feel, their balance. After half an hour, he was content.

He mounted up and rode on.

Sometime in the late afternoon he brought down a big jackrabbit with the Winchester. He ate at dusk, protected by a rock behind him and a row of boulders before him. The firelight would reflect, of course, but he did not intend to cook very long, just enough so he could eat.

When the meat was done he poured dirt on the fire and went away a few yards, where he settled his spine against a rock and ate. His coffee had been made; he sipped it as he smoked and ran his eyes across the land.

Might be a good idea to ride into Paydirt after dark, just to see where Bledsoe had put Kate. He doubted that the outlaw would take her with him across the countryside. Bledsoe would want to keep her hidden, but available. And alive. She was no use to him dead. He wanted her half brother, not the girl.

He mounted up by starlight and rode down off the hills to the flatland. After a time he made out the lights of the town, gleaming dully in the darkness of the night. He sat his saddle and watched those lights for a long time. Once in a while he saw a man cross the street and enter the saloon.

He toed the dun to a walk and eased his way around Paydirt, just observing it. He could hardly ride in. Rawhide Bledsoe had adopted Paydirt as his town. It would take a lot of guns to force him out.

Carty was about to move closer when three men came out of the saloon and mounted up, turned their horses, and rode away. Carty knew two of those by sight. One was Waco Jimmy Blackwood, another was one of those who had come at him from behind when they had trapped him.

He smiled coldly. They were riding easily, with no thought of anything in their minds, probably, but their bedrolls and sleep. He walked the dun on soft ground, and when the wind shifted so that it blew in his face, he cantered. He trailed them for an hour, until he drew rein at sight of a campfire.

There were four men about the fire. Two of them were unrolling their blankets; another man was standing, staring down into the flames, with one more pushing wood onto the flames.

The man who had been tending the fire as his friends rode up, asked, "Bledsoe still mulish?"

"Like a wounded bear." Waco Jimmy paused and chuckled. "Carty sure threw lead. I never saw a man get so many shots off so fast."

Another man grunted. "We were shooting at him, too."

"Good thing. He maybe would have had us all, we hadn't had guns in our hands."

"Glad he's dead. That man still sends chills up my spine."

Carty waited until the men were in their blankets, rolled up near the fire. Then he swung down from the saddle carefully, making no sound. He lifted out the Winchester and stood beside the dun, stroking its nose. Not until he heard snores did he ease forward, walking carefully to make no sound.

Their saddles were off to one side, with their rifles in the scabbards. Carty gave them a glance but did not pause in his walking. He moved closer, until he was standing over their blanketed bodies.

He swung his toe and kicked one man awake.

The man opened his eyes. Those eyes got bigger and bigger, and his mouth fell open. Carty put the muzzle of the Winchester close to his chest and said softly, "You make a sound, you're a dead man."

The man nodded.

"Stand up, nice and slowly. Unbuckle your gunbelt and toss it over to one side."

The man did as he was told. Quietly, as though afraid the slightest sound might make Carty's trigger finger move, he stood up and unbuckled his gunbelt, heaving it. Carty waggled the Winchester at him.

"Go over there and stand with your arms up." He added, "You bring those arms down and I shoot."

Carty woke them all, one after the other, and disarmed them. Only Waco Jimmy Blackwood showed any signs of fight. He hesitated with his hands before the buckle of his gunbelt, and his eyes glinted as though he were calculating his chances.

"Go on," Carty said softly. "See if you can beat my bullet."

The Winchester was aimed right at his middle. Waco Jimmy looked at it, raised his eyes to study Carty, then shrugged. "You got me covered," he muttered.

Carty dropped the rifle and stood waiting.

"You're not covered now. Do what you want."

Blackwood drew a deep breath. This man before him stood with his hands at his sides, just watching. But there was something animal-like in his eyes, something cold and hard, that Blackwood did not like.

He muttered, "I'm going to loosen my shellbelt."

When the shellbelt was at his feet, he picked it up and tossed it, then went to stand with his friends. Carty lifted the Winchester and held it in his left hand.

"You boys want to go back to Paydirt? Or do you want to ride out of here—and stay out?"

Waco Jimmy snarled, "We'll take Paydirt."

"Start walking."

One of the others yelped, "Walk?"

"All the way. Start moving. And tell Bledsoe I'll be coming for him soon as I decide he's lived long enough."

He watched them walk out, waiting until they were distant specks before he moved. One by one he broke their rifles over a rock, then lifted their gunbelts and draped them across his saddlehorn. He gathered the tie ropes of the horses and carried them toward the dun.

He mounted up and rode away, the four horses trotting after him. There was a little canyon back a ways; he would leave the horses there and go on to make his lonely camp a few miles from there.

Tomorrow night he would visit Paydirt.

CHAPTER 11

Rawhide Bledsoe knew the bite of anger. He stood on the porch of the Paydirt saloon and stared off across the flatland toward the mountains. That woman he had taken, who was in an upstairs room right now, troubled him.

Originally, he had meant to kill her, or hold her to bring Morgan Chance out into the open, where he could get at him. Now that he had taken her prisoner, something inside him rebelled at killing her. He was not a man who warred with women. If it came right down to it, he wasn't at all sure he could kill her. No matter how much he hated her brother.

Oh, he might cuff her around a little, but as for killing—well, he wasn't too happy about that. No man who thought anything of himself harmed a woman, out here. Still, he could use her as a bargaining point, to get Morgan Chance to show himself.

For the last couple of days, he had begun to wonder. Chance hadn't done a damn thing. No riders had come looking for the girl, nobody had made any inquiries. Seemed almost as if Morg Chance was glad to be rid of her. But that was nonsense, of course.

He was turning away when he saw the seven men in the distance, walking toward the town. They limped, they made painful progress, and one or two of them were staggering.

Rawhide Bledsoe shouted a curse and stepped off the porch, moving to meet them. He noted that they had no rifles, that no handguns caused their holsters to sag.

"What the hell happened?" he bellowed.

Waco Jimmy Blackwood snarled, "We met Carty!"

Bledsoe halted, stiffening. A coldness ran down his spine, and a pulse beat faster in his thick neck. His eyes studied each man, saw the dust on their clothes, the tiredness in their faces. It looked as if they had walked all night.

"Thought you'd finished him," he said flatly.

"Thought so myself. We didn't. He was shot full of holes, but he managed to live. Been a couple of weeks since then. He's had time to recover, more or less. He looked healthy enough last night."

The story came out, interjected here and there with curses. Bledsoe listened, not speaking, but feeling again that coldness settling inside him. Amos Carty was like a shadow off somewhere around Paydirt, and he had a score to even—with him, with Rawhide Bledsoe.

He led the way to the saloon.

"You boys get some rest and some guns. Carty'll come here, looking for the girl. We want to be ready for him."

He had eleven men, besides himself. They were firmly established in Paydirt now; they just about ran the town. No one man—not even Carty—could do very much about that. The trouble was, Carty was like no man Rawhide Bledsoe had ever known. He might be a white man, but he thought and acted like an Indian. You couldn't figure on him.

Except that he would try to get the girl. That was his weakness; he would have to play up to it.

He waited until the four men had gone up the staircase to the bedrooms, then he turned and went into the saloon.

Lou Brent was there, riffling a pack of cards. Bledsoe pulled out a chair and seated himself.

"We're in trouble, Lou," he said heavily. "Carty's still alive."

Lou Brent stilled his hands that held the cards. His eyes were bright as they studied the face of this big man who sat across from him. "Thought the boys finished him off when they got the girl."

"So did I. So did they. They didn't."

Brent sighed. "Changes things."

"Not that much. What can one man do against all of us?"

"It was him found Waco and the others, wasn't it? Saw them come in without their guns. They're lucky to be alive."

"How do you know it was Carty?"

"Figures. Who else could do a thing like that?"

"We still got the girl."

"Not for long, not if Carty wants her."

"What can he do?"

"I don't know, Rawhide. But I don't like it. Be a good idea if we just up and rode to Chessboard and finished off Morg Chance. Then we could ride out, and Carty wouldn't bother to come after us."

"No. I'll pick the place, the time. But I got to get word to Chessboard. If Chance isn't looking for his sister, I got to tell him where she is."

"Who you figure on sending?"

Bledsoe smiled faintly. "The doc, maybe."

Brent nodded. "Makes sense. He might get the job done. Then we'll fort up here and be ready for them—if Chance comes, that is."

"What you mean by that?"

Lou Brent shrugged. "Seems to me Chance doesn't care what happens to that girl."

Bledsoe rubbed his unshaven jaw. "You think that too, huh? Could be. Without her, he'd get to keep that ranch, most likely. Got to think about that."

Lou Brent riffled the cards and began to deal them. Bledsoe watched the cards fall into neat little piles. He badly wanted a drink.

Night was soft across the land, with a half moon shining down on the ocotillo shrubs and the cactus spines. Shadows lay where those plants grew, forming splotches of blackness across the ground. Once in a while, a small bit of that darkness moved, always closer to the buildings.

A tinny piano made sound in Paydirt, and Amos Carty could hear a girl laugh. There were the voices of men, too, raised in conversation, and once in a while, someone cursed. They would be playing poker in the saloon; everyone would be busy, at one thing or another.

Carty moved slowly. He was in no haste.

He was angling his crawl for the stable, because what he wanted was in the stable, or so he thought. He could make out the horses in the corral attached to it, but he was upwind from the horses, they couldn't scent him. As old Buffalo Horn had taught him, he moved slowly, carefully, without sound.

When he came to the stable wall, he hugged its base, one more dark shadow merging with the others. He lay there, listening. Satisfied that no one was inside, he crawled on. When he reached the open doorway, he slid inside and rose carefully to his feet.

He found the saddles after a time. He went from one to another until he came upon his own—a scratch across the skirt, a nick on the horn where a bullet had hit, long ago, and he knew it. Very carefully he felt around, discovering his bedroll. His warbag should be here, close by.

When he found it, he opened it and reached inside. His fingers went over his Kiowa moccasins, and his lips twitched into a smile. In moments he had shed his boots and slipped on the moccasins.

His eyes studied the buildings as he stood in the dark stable. Easy enough to pick out the saloon, with the lights shining. Farther down the street was a blacksmith shop and what might pass for a stable. Carty considered the buildings.

Kate Macklin would be in the saloon, upstairs. She would be in one of the bedrooms, maybe with a guard before her door. The thing to do would be to find out which room she was in, if he could manage that. It wouldn't be easy.

He stepped from the stable and ran across the open space until he was in the shadows of the building wall. The sounds from the saloon were louder now, but he shut his mind to them as his eyes studied the windows on the second floor. Kate Macklin was in one of those rooms, he felt almost certain. If she were alive.

Carty found a barrel, mounted on it, and reached upward until he could catch hold of the overhang. He lifted easily onto it, just below the line of windows. Flat on his belly, he raised his head and sought to peer in a window. He could see nothing.

Carefully, making no sound, he moved on.

Someone was breathing inside the room of the fourth window. Carty heard it and lay flat, listening. Someone was sleeping in this room, he felt certain. Raising his hand, he ran it over the sill. The window was open an inch or two.

Gently, he raised the window.

"Kate," he whispered. "Kate!"

The breathing stopped, then began again.

"Kate."

A bedspring creaked.

"Kate."

Someone gasped. The bedsprings creaked once more, and now he heard a floorboard sound an echo. Then Kate Macklin was at the window, staring at him, a hand to her throat, her face white, and her eyes enormous.

"You!" she breathed. "But I saw you shot. I thought you were dead."

"Well, I'm not. You dressed?"

Her head nodded.

"Can you climb out that window?"

"I can get out, but they'll come after me. After us."

"What I want them to do," he chuckled coldly.

There was something in his voice that made her shiver. She put a leg over the sill, saw him slide away to give her room, and then she swung out onto the overhang. She lay flat as he was doing and crawled along, his face only inches from hers.

She lay there and watched him swing down off the overhang onto a barrel. She crawled on, backed up, and let her legs dangle. Her muscles ached with the strain of holding on, but then his hands were on her legs and he was guiding her downward, gripping her.

"No noise," he cautioned.

His hand caught hers, and brought her across the space between the saloon-hotel and the stable. They moved along the wall until they were at the open doorway. Carty went inside and came out carrying a rifle and a pair of worn boots. He nodded at her, and she turned and moved along the wall until the stable hid them from any curious eyes in the saloon.

"We crawl now," he told her. "And—slowly."

It took them a long time because Carty insisted that they aim their bodies for the shadows of the ocotillo and the cactus. Each time they reached one of those dark splotches, he made her wait while he looked back at the town.

Not until they were close to half a mile away, where clumps of organ-pipe cactus lifted their arms to the sky, did Carty permit the girl to rise to her feet. They stood watching the town; they heard the sounds of the piano, faint with distance.

Carty said, "All right, we walk. Got a horse tethered not far away."

Kate looked at him and saw his face shadowed by moonlight under the Plains hat. "Did my brother send you?" she asked.

"Came alone, on my own. You think Morg wants you back?"

Kate gasped. "What—what do you mean?"

"Only one thing Morg wants. Your ranch. Sooner you understand that, the better off you'll be."

She thought about that as she walked. Oh, she knew there was no love lost between Morgan and herself, but he was her brother—half brother, that is. She knew nothing about Carty, even less than she did about Morgan, but there was something about Carty, some quality, that made him seem like an old friend. She realized suddenly, and with something of a shock, that if it came to a choice between her half brother and Amos Carty, she would choose this man whom others called the Indian.

She asked now, "What difference does it make to you who owns Chessboard?"

"None at all. My business is with your brother—and with Bledsoe, too, because his men shot me down. Right now, though, I got to see you safe."

"Safe," she exclaimed bitterly. "Where can I be safe around here?"

"Little canyon I know. Now, just keep on walking. Sooner or later they're going to find you're gone, and they'll start looking. We want to be ready for that."

Half a mile farther on, they came up on the dun. The horse pricked up its ears and whinnied faintly. Carty tied his boots to the saddle thongs and kept the Winchester rifle in his hand.

"You mount up. We got a piece to travel yet."

Kate protested, but Carty merely gestured, and she put a foot in the stirrup and swung into the saddle. She walked the horse, watching Carty move along, off to one side, the rifle in his hands, his trigger finger in the guard. At the slightest sound, she knew, he would be ready to fire.

Oddly enough, she felt very safe with him.

Dawn was in the air when Carty led the way into a small canyon. Kate could see four horses below, cropping grass. Carty watched her dismount, then unsaddled the dun and tied a long rope to its halter. He walked away, lifted up a blanket, and rolled himself up in it.

"You can finish sleeping now, you want," he told her.

He lay down on the ground. Instantly, or so it seemed to the girl, he was asleep. She watched him, studied the lines of his face. There was weariness in it, and marks of remembered pain. Kate busied herself picking up bits and lengths of dried wood. When he woke, he might want a fire.

It was late afternoon when she heard the hoofbeats. She had slept for a time, awakened to glance over at Carty, then settled back to sleep. But the sounds of those approaching horses drove all thought of sleep away.

She turned toward Carty to awaken him.

He was on his feet, moving away, the rifle still in his hands. He said softly, "Get over behind those rocks. And don't you move, girl."

He disappeared between two boulders. Kate ran for the rocks he had indicated, head down. She was too slow. Out of the corners of her eyes she saw three men on horses swing up over the top of a ridge. One of those men pointed an arm at her and shouted something.

A bullet kicked dust at her racing feet. Kate stumbled and fell headlong.

"We got her dead to rights," somebody shouted.

"Might be we'll have some fun before we finish her. Morg didn't say nothin' about that."

Fear was an iciness inside her. She could not have moved, no matter what happened. Her only hope was Carty.

She heard saddle leather creak. The men were dismounting, approaching her. Where was Carty? What was he doing?

"Far enough," Carty's voice said, coldly.

A man cursed. Kate lifted her head and stared. None of them was paying any mind to her.

Carty was rising from those rocks toward which he had run. He was standing with his arms by his sides; there was no sign of the rifle. He seemed almost unconcerned, yet Kate thought suddenly that she had never seen anything look more dangerous.

"Ken Stevens was a friend of mine," Carty said softly. "I heard he was dry-gulched by three men. One of them was you, Pike."

Pike Shattuck stared at Carty, disbelief in his eyes. He knew that the Indian had set out after Rawhide Bledsoe and the men who had shot him and left him for dead.

What was he doing here, with Kate? Bledsoe had taken Kate. Could the Indian have freed her, gotten her away from Bledsoe and his men? Didn't seem likely. He would have bet against it. But they were here, together.

"Any time, Pike. You others, too."

One of the three men licked his dry lips. "We got no quarrel with you, Carty."

"Hell you ain't. You ride with Morg. That's enough."

Pike Shattuck said, "You going to take us all on when—"

His hand dropped for his gun. Pike Shattuck had always considered himself a better than average hand with a six-gun. He was no Hickok or Hardin, but he had two men almost as good beside him, and—

Carty's hands blurred. They fell and they came up with the Patterson Colts, and he was throwing himself sideways even as those guns spat red flame. He hit the ground and rolled over onto his feet, and his shots were spaced so swiftly they sounded almost as one.

Pike Shattuck felt the shock of two bullets going into his chest. He teetered there, the gun in his hand a heavy weight. He fell face forward. He did not see the men on either side of him, he did not know that Carty's third bullet had caught Luke Benjamin in the throat, tearing half of it away. Nor did he see Rufe Jackson take the fourth bullet in his midsection.

Pike Shattuck was dead before he struck the ground.

Luke Benjamin was dead too, his throat spurting blood.

Only Jackson still lived, but the bullethole in his midsection was like a red-hot dagger lancing through him. His gun fired into the ground even as another bullet from Carty's gun drove into his chest. He swayed sideways, then toppled. He shook a moment, his body arched upward, and then relaxed.

Kate Macklin came off the ground, heart thumping, mouth dry. Her eyes went over the three men, then turned to look at Amos Carty.

"You—"

She could not form the words. She swallowed, and touched her tongue to her lips. Again she fought to make herself heard.

"You killed them all," she whispered.

"Them or me. And you."

She walked toward him, stumbling a little. He watched her come, lifting bullets from his shellbelts and thumbing them into the empty chambers. Her hands went out and caught his arm. The muscles of that arm were like steel beneath her fingers.

"They would have killed me, I think," she whispered.

He nodded. "Figured on it. Thought you were alone."

"There were—three of them."

Carty smiled faintly. He found his memory carrying him backward over the years, to the long hours of practicing his draw, of leaping sideways and still shooting. How could he tell of the pain of aching muscles, the iron will that drove him always to that steady practice, practice, practice? He had been gifted with fast hands, with unusual co-ordination. He had built that speed and that facility of muscle into what he had become.

"They saw only one man. Made them a little too confident."

Her eyes were on his own. Slowly, she shook her head. "No. It was you. I've seen you shoot before, but—never like that."

He shrugged and holstered his guns. "A man does what he has to."

She turned her stare to the bodies. "What about them?"

"We'll send them back to Morg."

Kate started. "To my brother?"

"Got to let him know about Bledsoe, don't we? He'll think Bledsoe did it. Force Morg to make his move. Can't have him just sitting on that ranch like a spider in its web."

He moved away from the girl toward the dead bodies, saying over his shoulder, "Morg's going to think Bledsoe and his boys did this shooting, that they caught Shattuck and the others, picked them off."

He began to work, lifting one of the bodies, getting it into the saddle. The horse shied, but Carty whispered to it, and after a time, it quieted. When the body was in the kak, Carty took the lariat hanging from the horn and tied the body securely.

One after the other he fastened those bodies in the saddles.

He found a bit of paper in a saddlebag and looked at Kate Macklin.

"Can you print words?"

Kate started. "Of course."

From a pocket he brought out the stub of a pencil, handing the pencil and the paper to the girl. "Write 'Waiting in Paydirt.' That's all. Print it."

Kate moved to a rock and rested the paper on it. She printed carefully, then gave the paper back to Carty. He looked down at what she had written, and it came to her that this man could not read.

Well, that was not so surprising. Many men in the West could not read, could not write. Many could not even sign their names.

"You can't read that, can you?" she asked gently.

He nodded. "I can read. My pop taught me." He glanced sideways at the girl. "You got a pin on you?"

She laughed, fumbled at her blouse, and handed him the pin.

Carty walked with the pin and the paper to the body of

Pike Shattuck. He stepped into the stirrup and pinned the note to Shattuck's shirt. Then he stepped down, put Shattuck's left boot back in the stirrup, and went from horse to horse, slapping each across the rump.

The horses trotted off. Carty said almost to himself, "Those broncs will head back to Chessboard. They're Chessboard stock. Morg will see them coming in. After that—" He shrugged. "We got to hope."

Kate sat down on a rock, looking at him. "You want them to fight. You want Morgan to ride into that Paydirt town and meet with that man called Bledsoe."

"Only way to handle it."

"It seems so cold-blooded. You want those men to kill each other."

"Saves me the trouble."

She looked at him wonderingly. "How can you play with men's lives that way?"

Carty stared at her, head tilted slightly so that his Plains hat put a shadow across his eyes. "You want your ranch back?"

"Well—yes, of course."

"Won't be yours as long as Morg's alive."

She thought about that, studying at the toes of her scuffed boots. She kicked a pebble and watched it bounce. "But those others, the men in Paydirt?"

"You mean you don't bear them any ill will, after what they done to you?"

She flushed. "Yes, of course. I'm no plaster saint, you know. But it seems so—so heartless, to plan for men to kill each other the way you're doing."

"Some men need killing, ma'am. The only thing they understand."

She could hardly argue with that, she knew.

Morgan Chance was at the horse corral with a lariat in his hand and a roan gelding in the loop when he saw the dust. He eyed that dust a moment—three horses, walking slowly. Men in the saddle, too. Tired men. They slumped forward, and one of them seemed about to fall.

"Hobe," he yelled. "Hobe, take a look."

Hobe Talbert ran from the smithy where he had been hammering at a horseshoe. He went past the corral and the bunkhouse and out onto the grass before he slid to a halt. There was something wrong about those riders, something unnatural.

"It's Pike," he bellowed. "Pike and Luke and Rufe!"

He ran.

Behind him, Morgan Chance knew the keen bite of fear. He knew without looking more closely that those three men were dead. Those three men were hard men, or had been. Each of those men had killed other men in his time. Each one was a hardcase. Somebody had dry-gulched them.

He went after Hobe at the run, his mouth dry.

When he was close enough, he saw that those men had been shot from the front, with what looked to be revolver bullets. But how could that be? He could not imagine Shattuck letting himself be caught in any trap, where men with revolvers would shoot them down.

Hobe Talbert was swearing softly.

"Don't make sense," he muttered.

"There's some sort of paper pinned to Pike."

Morgan Chance read that paper, and his face paled slightly. "Bledsoe," he whispered. "It was Bledsoe and his boys. By God! They won't get away with this, Hobe."

"Seems funny, somehow," Talbert said. "Pike wasn't

likely to be caught in any trap, less'n some men were waiting in ambush for him and the others."

They lifted the men down when the horses had walked to the corral, and they stood staring at their bodies on the ground. Some of his uneasiness was leaving Morgan Chance, to be replaced by a deep, hard fury.

"It was Bledsoe," he muttered. "Damn him!"

Hobe Talbert scratched his ear. "Not so sure about that, Morg. That's awful good shooting, there. Five shots. One in Rufe's belly, one in his heart. Only one in Luke, that tore half his throat away. Two in Pike, right about where his heart ought to be, had he one."

Morgan Chance eyed his companion. "You trying to say something?"

"One man," Hobe offered hesitantly.

"*One* man? You loco?"

"Their guns been fired. All 'cept Pike's. He never did get his shot off. Don't reckon they hit anything, though."

"Nobody could gun down Pike Shattuck, Jackson, and Benjamin, not in a fair fight."

"Carty might."

"*Carty?*" For an instant, Morgan Chance stood frozen. Then he grunted, "What I said still goes. You're loco."

Talbert grinned. "Mebbe so. What you going to do?"

"Ride into Paydirt, like we're invited. I'm going to shoot up that town—or whoever's inside it."

"Bledsoe?"

"That's what I'm thinking."

Hobe Talbert shrugged. He had known this day was coming, ever since they had ridden out of Stovepipe. He was a little surprised that it had not come sooner. He reached down and tore the sheet of paper from Shattuck's vest.

"A woman printed that," he offered. "It's neat, sort of fancy."

"Kate."

Hobe Talbert looked surprised. "Hadn't thought about that. Mebbe you're right—about Bledsoe and not Carty doing that shooting. Bledsoe has Kate. He's keeping her alive to get you to go after her."

"Not going after Kate."

Hobe chuckled. "Be too bad if she stopped a bullet during the fighting, wouldn't it?"

"During or after, it makes no difference."

Morgan Chance walked away from the corral and the three bodies. He was going to have to send for the rest of his boys, camped out there in the hills. He wanted all his guns with him when he went into Paydirt. He meant to get Rawhide Bledsoe before Bledsoe could whittle down his men one by one, from ambush.

Hobe watched him walk away, an uneasy feeling in his middle. Maybe it had been Bledsoe who had done away with Shattuck and the other two, Bledsoe and his men. But those shots were too well placed for his liking. If they'd been shot from ambush, there should be other wounds in their bodies.

Not many men could shoot that well, with either a handgun or a rifle. No wasted shots, no minor wounds. Each one of those wounds could be mortal.

Carty? Could the Indian shoot that well? Hobe had the uncomfortable feeling that he could. But one man, against Pike and Luke and Billy? Didn't seem likely.

He went to get a spade to dig three graves. As he walked, he wondered who would dig his grave when he died.

CHAPTER 12

Carty was up and moving about when Kate woke. She lay and studied his easy movements, his grace of body. He was much like a wild animal, she thought, not for the first time, but there was something about him that she could be content with. A land like this bred men such as Amos Carty. A good thing for her, too.

She threw back her blanket. "I'll make the coffee."

He turned his head and studied her. "Waiting for that. You got to teach me the trick. Mine's like dirty water, sometimes."

"Use more coffee," she smiled.

He had skinned two hares, she saw. Now, when had he shot those? She took them from him, caught up the handful of herbs he had pulled, and brought them to the fire. In moments, when she caught the aroma of cooking meat, her mouth began to water. She hadn't realized she had been so hungry.

They ate side by side. When they were done, Carty looked at her, saying, "You stay here. You understand? Don't you move."

He rose and kicked dirt on the fire. "And don't make another fire. Don't want anyone finding you."

"Oh? And what are you going to do?"

"Ride into Paydirt."

Her eyes opened wide. "They'll be waiting for you. Not

only Bledsoe and his men, but my brother, too. They'll shoot you down on sight, all of them."

His grin was wry, amused. "Not if things work out the way I've planned." He hesitated, then said, "Nobody knows I'm the one got you out of there. They may do some guessin', but they won't be sure. I'll be all right. I'll make it my business to play it safe."

He saddled the dun, his movements swift and sure, without waste. He put a foot into the stirrup and swung up. He looked down at her, and his face was cold and hard.

"You stay put, now," he told her.

She nodded, asking, "You will be back?"

"If I'm alive."

He rode away into the morning sunlight, and Kate watched him until he disappeared over the rim of the canyon. She walked back toward the rock overhang to seat herself on a chunk of malpais. She felt very lonely.

Carty rode into Paydirt, easing the dun down the main street, without troubling himself to hide. He feared no bullet—not at the moment, at least. The bullets would come, but not for a time. A man stood at the entrance to the little saloon, watching him.

Carty was almost at the tierail when the man turned and went in through the batwings. Carty was amused. The man was carrying word to Bledsoe. Well, let him. He himself was going in there to confront Bledsoe, to bring everything to a head. His cabin in the Wind River country was waiting; he wanted to be off on the grulla and riding northward in another day or two.

He walked into the saloon as might a man who had no worry in his mind. He moved toward the bar and nodded his head at Bledsoe and at Lou Trent, who sat beside him at a table. Bledsoe was scowling, but Trent was poised and alert, waiting.

"Whatever you have," Carty told the bartender.

Bledsoe said softly, "You come for the girl, you're too late. She got away."

Carty nodded. "I owe somebody for taking that girl away from me. I owe somebody for filling me full of lead and leaving me there to die."

The bartender slid the glass across the bar toward him. Carty ignored it. His eyes flicked from one face to another. Waco Jimmy Blackwood was standing, his right hand poised above his gunbutt. He saw other faces, too— the two men who had been with Blackwood when they had taken Kate Macklin from him and left him for dead— and another man, the one who had come up behind him at that ambush.

They were waiting on Rawhide Bledsoe.

Carty smiled thinly. "Before we open the dance, I ought to warn you, Rawhide, Morgan Chance and his boys are coming in here today."

Somebody cursed. Rawhide Bledsoe looked suspicious, but Lou Trent leaned forward, fixing his gaze on Carty. "Now, how would you know that?" he asked softly.

"I set it up for you. Figuring I'd be doing you a favor, seeing as how you're sitting here not knowing how to hit out at him."

"How could you do that?" Bledsoe rasped.

"Met up with Pike Shattuck and two other men. Let them go for their guns, seeing that was what they wanted. After I'd killed them, I put them back in their saddles and tied them there; let their horses take them back to the ranch. I also wrote a little note, telling them I'd be waiting for them in Paydirt."

Bledsoe rose to his feet. "You did all that?"

"Hell, I don't believe it."

That was Waco Jimmy. Carty flicked his eyes at him. "Fact. We went for our guns. I was faster."

"You must have shot them in the back," a man laughed.

"Face to face. We all drew. They were a mite slow."

"No man is that fast."

Lou Trent chuckled. "Amos Carty is. I'd have liked to have seen that."

There was a little silence.

Carty said, "I've come for the girl, Bledsoe. I take her and ride out of here. I'll leave you and Morg to settle your differences.

"The girl's gone."

Carty laughed. It was a chilling laugh that sent ice down the backbones of the men who heard it.

Lou Trent said, "It's true enough. She busted out the back way and ran off. We had boys out hunting for her all night. We couldn't find her."

"We're going to look again today. She can't be far," growled Bledsoe.

Carty waited. After a moment he shifted his feet. "You really expect me to believe that?"

Bledsoe cursed. "It's true enough. I don't know how she did it, but she did."

"Not without help," Carty said softly, and looked from one man to another. "Wondering which of your boys might have decided to step out and let her go—that is, if you're telling the truth."

Bledsoe followed Carty's eyes, staring at each of his men. "I've ridden with these men a long time, Carty."

"Maybe you ain't as pretty as Kate Macklin."

Lou Brent asked, "What's your concern in all this,

Carty? Ain't like you to come in here with a warning, especially since it was our boys that took that girl away from you."

"Don't like to see any man shot down without a chance to defend himself."

"It's more than that."

"Then you figure it out." Carty waited, tensed and ready. It may have been a fool move on his part to come in here, but he was no man to hide behind his own actions. Rawhide Bledsoe was an outlaw and a killer, but so was Morgan Chance, and the way Carty looked at it, every man had a right to defend himself.

Besides, he told himself wryly, he was here to finish off what one or the other began. Kate Macklin had no chance at all with her brother or this big man named Bledsoe still alive. Carty was tired of this hot country; he wanted to be up there in Wyoming at his cabin. The sooner he got this show started, the better.

He said now, "You call it, Bledsoe. You want me, here I am. You may get me, but I'll get three or four of you—and you first. You want to wait for Chance, just tell me, and I'll stand aside."

Rawhide Bledsoe had the uncomfortable feeling that Amos Carty was laughing at him. Or maybe he was laughing at Fate.

"I got nothing against you. You can ride out," he muttered.

"I'll stay. I want to see what happens."

Carty turned his eyes on them all and studied them. They would make no trouble for him, not now. The time for that had passed. They were thinking about Morgan Chance right now, knowing he was coming, him and his riders. He eased away from the bar, carefully, his drink untouched.

He moved out into the sunlight and walked down the dusty street. His eyes scanned the hills to the east. Chessboard would be coming from the east, if they didn't circle around and hit town from some other direction. He wondered as he stood there whether Morgan Chance was that smart. Could be. In that case, Carty would have to be prepared.

He moved to the dun and lifted out his rifle. With the rifle in the crook of an arm, he stepped back into the shadows. It might be a long wait, and the sun was hot. He found a bench that let him prop his back against a building wall. He rolled a cigarette and lighted it, breathing in the smoke, letting it out slowly.

The town was very quiet. There was no sound, none at all. It was as if the buildings themselves were waiting, along with the men. He heard the batwings creak, the pound of boots on board and dirt. Carty smiled thinly. Bledsoe was sending out men to watch. Well, he had no quarrel with that. It was the smart thing to do.

He waited, patiently.

The sun crawled higher into the sky, and the heat made trickles of sweat run down his back. Where was Morgan Chance? He had to come here, there was no other way open to him, unless he was willing to see his men shot down whenever they rode away from Chessboard. Morg was no fool, whatever else he might be. It had come to this, to the showdown, if he wanted to keep what he had seemingly won.

Rawhide Bledsoe was like a burr under Morg's saddle. He had to get rid of him to have any peace whenever he wanted to ride around the ranch he was stealing. It had to be settled, one way or the other. Carty wondered if Macklin's lands, that flat-faced man who gave his name as Poke Drummond and young Billy Anderson, would be in

that war party Morg was bringing to Paydirt. He hoped
not. They were good men; Kate would need men like that
when this was over.

He shifted his position on the bench.

Might be a good idea to wander around, about now. He
wanted another look at those hills. He rose and moved
around behind the saloon, walking easily, carefully.

There was a bit of dust in the air, hanging there, slowly
settling. Carty eyed it. That dust cloud had been made
some time ago by a group of riders. Those riders should
be in view by now.

Carty moved swiftly, dropping to the ground and
crawling until he was behind a stone-walled well in back
of the livery stable. He waited then, listening. His eyes
roved the mesquite and the cactus, the ocotillo and the
cholla. There was no movement of any kind.

Then he saw a patch of brown. He waited, sliding the
Winchester forward. When the brown patch moved, he
sighted on it and curled his finger around the trigger. He
waited, as old Buffalo Horn had taught, until he could see
what it was he was shooting at. Only when he saw the
whiteness of a face did he ease back on the trigger.

A man screamed, rose up, and took two steps before
plunging forward onto his face. He did not move again.

But in the town there was a babble of voices, a few
curses, the sound of thudding boots. He had spoiled Morgan Chance's try for an ambush of sorts. That was all he
wanted at the moment. He slid backward, with the stone
well before him as a shield.

When he was inside the little space between the saloon
and the stable, he rose to his feet. Well, he had opened
the show. It was up to Morgan Chance and Rawhide
Bledsoe and their men, now.

Waco Jimmy Blackwood came around the far end of

the building, rifle in his hands. He saw Carty, and his rifle came up.

Carty fired twice.

Two reddish holes showed in Blackwood's shirt. He staggered sideways against the building wall. His eyes were wide open, and he forced a sickly smile.

"You figurin' on—gettin' us all?" he asked, then toppled over. He did not move again.

Carty dropped to the ground. He had done enough. It was time to step back and let the others do the fighting. He would not have shot at Waco Jimmy if he hadn't started it. But he had taken a fighting man away from each group. He put his back to the saloon wall and waited.

He did not wait long.

Already guns were opening up from the saloon and out there in the brush. Soon now it would be a free-for-all, with men shooting at any gun flash they could see or at a patch of color out there where certain colors were out of place.

After a time, Carty scowled, eying the sky where the sun was beginning its drop to the west. Those two forces could be here all week, the way things were going. Might be a good thing to nudge them into faster action.

Crawling along the base of the saloon, he wriggled his way toward the stables. As he slid inside, he saw that his Spencer rifle was still in its scabbard. Might be a good idea to take that along with him. The sound of its firing was slightly different from that of the Winchester.

He made his way up a ladder and into the loft, carrying both rifles. He went to the hoist door and peered out. He was up high; he had a good view of the cactus-studded hillside to the east.

Carty lay down, cradling the Winchester in his arms, waiting.

When he saw movement in among the cactus branches, he slid the rifle barrel forward, waiting. In time, that man moved again, and Carty laid the barrel on him, just touching his finger to the trigger. Again the man moved.

Carty fired.

The man slumped. Carty watched him for a time, but he did not move again. If his bullet had gone where he aimed it—and his bullets usually did—that man was dead with a hole in his head.

He slid back and went down the ladder. Taking the Spencer, he moved toward a window. There was no glass in that windowframe, just a length of burlap. He eased the burlap to one side and leaned against the barn wall.

A shadow touched a rear window of the saloon.

Carty put a bullet to one side of that shadow, where he glimpsed a shirt and vest. A man jerked and moved forward so that Carty could see the angle of his jaw. Carty had not lifted his cheek from the riflestock; he put another bullet into that jaw and heard a man scream thickly.

He waited, patient as any Kiowa.

Suddenly Rawhide Bledsoe was calling out, "Morg! Morg Chance! You hear me?"

From the creosote bushes and the cactus, a voice roared back, "I'm here. What you got to say to me?"

"Let's settle this out in the open, man-to-man. I owe you, Morg. I want to face you, out there in the street. Come walking, and we'll come to meet you."

"With a hidden gun to pick us off! You think I'm loco?"

"No hidden guns. All out and open."

There was a silence. A wind had sprung up, there

where the flats lay thick with growth. That wind came down off the hills, and it stirred the branches of the cholla and the peyote, bringing with it the faint drift of fragrant sagebrush. Here and there men stirred on those flats, men who turned and looked in one direction.

Morgan Chance rose to his feet.

"I'm coming, me and the boys. I expect to see you out on that street soon as I come into view."

"We'll be there, Morg."

Carty waited, the shadows of the barn hiding him from view. It was all coming down to this, to this meeting on the dusty street of a little town where no more than eight or nine people lived all year. Everything was focused here, all the killings, all the lies, all the hatred. Carty stretched in the late-afternoon heat and eyed the rear door of the saloon.

He did not trust Rawhide Bledsoe; for that matter, he did not trust Morgan Chance either. He could do little about Chance, but he could make certain that Bledsoe did not leave a rifleman in that saloon to pick off Morgan Chance when he came walking in.

He heard a batwing door swing.

He ran across the open ground and slid in through the door, a six-gun in one hand, the rifles in the other. He paused with his back to a wall, listening. There was no sound. On his moccasined feet he moved forward, foot by foot.

A man was kneeling by a window, a rifle in his hands. He was watching the trail into town by which Morgan Chance and his men would come. Carty did not know his name, but he had been with Waco Johnny Blackwood when Bledsoe's men had cut him down and taken Kate Macklin from him.

Carty cocked his Patterson Colt.

The sound of that cocking was loud in the still saloon. The man by the window turned his head, staring. His face paled slightly under its tan.

"You sit put, mister. You put down that rifle nice and easy, and you unbuckle your shellbelt and kick it over this way."

The man licked his lips. All he need do was swing the barrel of his Winchester sideways to get off a shot. Yet the barrel of the Colt was fixed on his chest, and he knew he could not do it—not in time, anyhow. He put down the rifle very gently, and then he worked at the buckle of his gunbelt.

He slid them toward Carty.

"You go into the middle of the room and lie face down, with your arms stretched out. You move and I'll put lead into you."

"Chance will have somebody out there," the man protested.

"I'll handle him. You lie down."

When the man was on the floor, Carty stepped to a window. He had a good view of the flats; he could see Morg with his boys moving toward the town. He slid his eyes off them and turned his gaze to the ocotillo and the cactus, waiting.

In time, before Chance and his men had taken a dozen steps, he saw movement. A man was lying belly down behind a many-branched bitterbush, sunlight glinting off his rifle barrel. He was watching Morg move forward and was inching his rifle forward, very slowly.

Carty turned his head. The man he had disarmed was lying very still. Carty whispered, "You move and you're a dead man. Remember that."

He eased the Winchester forward and caught the waiting man in his sights. He fixed his attention on the man behind the bitterbush, but his ears listened to the man on the floor. The slightest drag of shoe across wood, the scrape of cloth, would have alerted him.

The marksman put his cheek to his riflestock. He poked the barrel between the stems of the bitterbush.

Carty fired.

The man rose up to his knees, mouth open. Carty could see blood on his shirt where his bullet had gone in. He also saw Morgan Chance whip around, staring.

"Fair fight," he shouted. "I got the man Bledsoe hid in here, Chance. You boys are on your own, now."

The man on the floor had turned his head and was staring at him. Carty chuckled. "Cheer up. At least you're going to live, if you behave yourself."

"Mind if I watch?" the man asked hoarsely.

"Come ahead."

The man rose to his feet, went to a window, and peered out. He was licking his lips, opening and closing his hands.

"You want to join your friends? I got no objections."

The man hesitated, then shook his head.

Morgan Chance and his men were at the edge of town now. They fanned out as they walked. Rawhide Bledsoe and his own men—there were eight of them, Carty noted —were also spreading out.

Somewhere off in the hills, a bobcat screamed. The heat was intense, the shadows of the buildings black along the ground. Bledsoe and his men waited as Morgan Chance advanced, kicking up little puffs of dust at every stride. Carty could see dark sweatstains on shirts, and here and there that sweat made little ridges on dust-covered faces.

Morgan Chance was passing the general store now, walking more slowly, flexing and unflexing his fingers.

Bledsoe waited, hands at his sides. Little Lou Brent stood to his right, absolutely motionless.

When they were fifty feet apart, Morgan Chance halted.

"Any time," he said softly.

Rawhide Bledsoe went for his gun.

Instantly the air was filled with sound. Flame ran from the gun muzzles, and here and there men jerked, staggered, and began to fall. Rawhide Bledsoe was backing up, blood on his shirt. Morgan Chance was on his knees, both hands holding the Colt with which he was aiming, firing.

Two bullets hit Chance and drove him backward onto the ground. His body lifted upward spasmodically, then he fell back and lay there, the dust settling on his body.

Bledsoe was down, too, his gun fallen from a hand. He was trying to crawl for that gun, but he never made it. Even with his hand outstretched, his fingers almost touching the butt, he stiffened and then went limp.

Men lay here and there in contorted attitudes.

Only Lou Brent was still standing, looking about him at the bodies, out of long habit reaching to his shellbelt to put more bullets in his gun. His hat had either fallen off or been shot from his head, and the sunlight touched the deep black of his long-uncut hair. He seemed dazed, and when he had loaded his guns, he drew a deep breath.

"Carty," he called.

Amos Carty pushed away from the window, motioning with a hand to the man beside him, who seemed stunned. "You go first, *amigo*."

They walked out into the sunlight, and Carty stood on the saloon porch, the two rifles in his left hand. His right hand hung near his gunbutt.

"I'm here, Lou."

"You played hell."

"I wanted a fair fight."

Brent nodded. His eyes left Carty to look about him at the bodies. He sighed and glanced again at the man on the porch.

"Nothing to keep me here any more," he said slowly.

"Nor me. You want help to bury them?"

Lou Brent shrugged. "Might as well. Then I'll have me a drink and ride out." He hesitated, then asked, "It was you who warned us, Carty? I'm obliged."

"Figured it would be best as an even break."

Brent considered that, eyes sharp. "In any sort of an even break, not many would be left alive."

"Figured that, too."

Brent walked to his hat, picked it up, and ran his eyes over the bullethole near the crown. "You got Chance and Bledsoe to do your work for you."

"Something like that."

Carty turned and walked along the dusty street. He peered down into faces, seeing them twisted in death or calm, as if sleep held them. One by one he examined them, and then he walked out among the cactus and the ocotillo. He came back after a time, and there was an urgency in his walk.

Brent was carrying a couple of shovels. The man who had been in the saloon was lifting a body to put it across a horse. "What is it?" he asked quietly.

"Hobe Talbert. They're all here but him."

Brent shrugged. "He ran off."

Carty led the grulla from the corral and saddled it. He swung up into the saddle. "I'll be back to bury Chance and his men," he said, and toed the grulla into a run.

He let the horse go, and the grulla was fast. It had a need for running in its muscles; it had been cooped a long time in that corral. It went fast, yet not fast enough for Carty, so he scratched its hide with the tip of his spur. The startled grulla settled into a killing pace.

As he came to the edge of the canyon, Carty reined up. He walked the horse now, using his eyes. When he saw the saddled horse near the edge of the rock overhang where he had left Kate, he slid from the saddle and moved forward on his moccasined feet, making no sound.

Kate Macklin was backed against the rock with Hobe Talbert standing there, grinning at her.

"We're just goin' to have a little fun, you and me, Kate. No need to—"

"Hobe."

Carty did not quite whisper the word, but he said it softly. Yet Talbert heard it and whirled around. Carty studied him almost lazily.

"They're dead, Hobe," he murmured softly. "All the others. Morg and the rest. They're waiting for you."

"Wha-what do you mean—they're waitin' for me?"

Talbert swallowed hard. He could read death in the face of this man whose gun hand had never been beaten. His tongue came out to moisten dry lips. He went for his gun.

Carty shot him three times, the shots sounding almost as one. Talbert stood a moment, blood seeping from three bloody holes in his chest. Then his legs buckled and he crumpled.

Carty looked at Kate. "You all right?" When she nodded and moved toward him, he said as he holstered his gun, "Morg's dead. He and Bledsoe shot it out in Paydirt."

He moved toward the grulla. "We can ride back to the ranch now. I'll take a buckboard and fetch Morg back for burying. I'll bury the others on that hill behind Paydirt."

He helped her into the saddle of Talbert's horse. She looked down at him and smiled faintly. "And after you do that? Will you come back to Chessboard?"

Carty stared off into the distance. Summer would be over soon, and there would be good hunting up there in Wyoming, come the fall. He wanted to taste deer meat cooked over his cabin fire, and smell the fragrance of the pines at sunset. He wanted to set his traps and walk the game trails, to drink from a cold mountain stream in the Wind River range.

He would bring back what was left of Morgan Chance to the ranch, he would bury the others. But one morning he would saddle up the grulla and he would ride out, just himself and the horse, and when the wild geese were flying south he would be in his cabin.

A man could ask no more of that in life.